THE VILLAIN & THE FORSAKEN

THE VILLAIN & THE FORSAKEN

BOOK I

VALE RAVENNA

THE VILLAIN & THE FORSAKEN
Published by VALE RAVENNA
www.valeravenna.com

Copyright © 2023 Vale Ravenna
ISBN 979-8-9894258-0-8

Cover design by Vale Ravenna.
Stock images: Deposit Photos.
Editing by Zainab M, romance editor at Heart Full of Reads Editing Services.

The Villain & the Forsaken is a dark gothic fantasy romance with elements that may be triggering to some readers. It includes kidnapping, captivity, and some physical abuse. It is intended for mature audiences, 18+. Read at your own risk.

To my mother, for shoving books into my little hands from the moment I could make out the meaning of words. I love you.

AUTHOR'S NOTE.

Hello, my beautiful readers!

As many of you know, I started my publishing journey with contemporary romance books penned as Valentina.

This story was originally written as a contemporary romance but as I wrote, I found myself wanting to give my characters supernatural abilities. After much inner exploration I understood what my soul was trying to tell me: get back to your roots.

I learned to read with books like The Hobbit and every Sherlock Holmes story I could get my sticky little hands on. It was the beginning of my love affair with fantasy and the gothic.

Old mansions, castles, dark and foggy worlds, pain and sorrow, all mixed with magic and epic battles between good and evil? Sign me up!

So, I took this previously contemporary story and reworked it, which led me to create a multi-realm world I am now deeply entrenched in.

The Realms of Anathema.

This novella is the beginning of it all, the first taste of this new world I hope you will love as much as I do.

As an Italian, I knew what my inspiration would be. Much of this world is inspired by Italian folklore, from angels to demons to the many stories Italian parents have shared with their children from generation to generation, often to spook us into obedience.

I also drew inspiration from the Ars Goetia, the first book of The Lesser Key of Solomon, an anonymous grimoire on demonology.

And because my mind works in crazy ways, some of the fashion and technology is inspired by aetherpunk which is like steampunk but with blue magic instead of steam.

So, without further ado, welcome to the world of the Realms of Anathema.

I hope you'll stay for a while.

Xoxo,

Vale

GLOSSARY

Mystic: A being with magical powers. Usually also immortal.

Mortal: A non-magical being with a normal, human, lifespan.

Aurora: the creator of all. Imagined by some as a light energy but by most as a Goddess.

The Stygian: a dark force born to counteract Aurora's utopian world. A darkness infecting land and Angels. Although non-corporeal, it is often referred to as its own entity.

The Abyss: the underworld, commonly called Hell.

The Auroran City: the place in the sky where Aurora and her Angels live, commonly called Heaven.

The Crystal Forest: A forest on The Island of Anathema. It's made of crystals carrying Aurora's life force, which keeps the realms alive.

Watchers: winged creatures assigned to care and protect Mystics. Each Watcher bonds with a specific Mystic they will go along with and serve for eternity.

Angels: created by Aurora, who made them to rule the world and watch over Mystics and mortals.

Demons: immortals spawned by the Stygian's dark powers. The first and most powerful demons being fallen Angels, who were lured by the darkness.

REETAH

"WITH ALL DUE RESPECT, YOUR HIGHNESS," the guard said, "your father would not be pleased with you walking home."

"Then don't tell him," Emmaline said, with a mischievous curl to her lips.

The guard turned to her. "But, ma'am, that—"

She put up a hand, effectively silencing him. "We're walking, and that's that."

His pursed lips and twisted face conveyed his frustration. But she was the princess, and besides the King and Queen, no one could tell her what to do.

Well, she also listened to me, but only when we were away from prying eyes and listening ears. It was uncouth to be best friends with your lady's maid.

I squeezed her arm. "I'm proud of you for speaking up for yourself."

Emmaline smiled, patting my hand. "You've taught me well."

There was a time when I envied my best friend, wishing I could be the one wearing the dresses I spent my days wriggling her into. Yearning to feel the weight of a gilded crown on my head. But the older we got, the further I walked from that notion.

Her life was stifling, and even though I wanted more out of my existence, "princess" was no longer one of my aspirations.

Instead, it comprised of becoming a Mystic. A being with incredible magical powers who got to have wings and ride around on an equally incredible winged Watcher. Whenever an Angel or Mystic went through their empowerment, the process through which their powers manifested, Goddess Aurora would gift a Watcher to them. Watchers were winged mystical creatures, such as gryphons, whose existence focused on transporting and protecting magical beings. They shared a telepathic bond with their charge and would do anything to protect them. Demons were the only magical creatures without Watchers as they were not created by Aurora, but by the dark power we referred to as the Stygian.

Of course, getting to fly atop a Watcher would never happen to me since I was a mortal lady's maid to an equally mortal princess.

"Reetah," Emmaline said, snapping her fingers in my face.

"I'm sorry, Your Highness."

Emmie, as I liked to call her, rolled her eyes. She didn't like her best friend addressing her in such a formal way, but I always did in front of others, especially those who would run to the king and tattle on me.

The King had always been kind, but he'd never treat me as his equal.

Emmie took me by the hand, pulling me along as we left Vestini's—our realm's capital and the place we called home—enormous community gardens. The crowds parted to let their princess through, each person bowing with the reverence she'd rightfully earned, as the kindest and most beautiful princess our realm of Frentani had ever known.

Emmie's parents weren't the best rulers. Not because they were cruel, but because they lacked motivation. Complacent and defeated was their way of life as they spent their days eating and drinking while complaining about the Stygian and the Angels' inability to eliminate it, because according to most mortals, this was solely the Angels' responsibility since they were the direct descendants of our Goddess.

The Stygian, the source of all darkness, was making the sun lose its potency, which brought in dark skies and too much rain. It was a serious problem since our realm survived on solar power for everything, plus crops suffered as the sun hid behind dense clouds for long periods. And so, over a millennia, the Stygian's sickness spread over the land like a deadly plague, causing parts of it to become ill, the soil turning black and barren.

I, for one, believed battling the Stygian's infection was everyone's responsibility. After all, we all ate the food our land provided.

I never understood why mortals had fought the Angels for control of the realms, only to sit on their asses and watch our world crumble.

Emmaline squeezed my arm, her posture tense and weary as she squinted at the gray sky with clouds so thick, they made our city bleak and terrifying.

The King had ordered the creation of artificial light as lanterns, which hung on tall posts lining each street, fashioning a soft amber glow above us.

Unfortunately, these lights were solar powered and their batteries were draining fast, as sunlight became a rarer occurrence.

I looked back at the two guards at our backs with their gloved hands resting on the hilts of their swords, ready to defend their princess, even though she was in no danger, and never had been.

The lanterns flickered one, two, three times, until they gave out, plunging us into a titanium gray I'd never seen before.

"It's getting worse," Emmaline whispered, gripping my hand with a painful strength. "Eventually, the sky will be pitch-black. I wonder if my father will spring into action then, when it's too dark and too late to save his realm."

"I'm sorry, Emmie," I said, my free hand patting her arm.

My heart constricted as scenes of crops dying and people losing their minds to hunger crossed my mind. Violence borne out of desperation was the most dangerous kind. It corroded, corrupted, and consumed people's souls until death and destruction were all that remained.

It was a not-so-distant future, and yet the king ate his way through it all, while his queen waded in a pool of complacency and hopelessness.

Such bleakness was breathtaking in the most disheartening way.

I was used to our mundane lives. Every day was the same here. I got up each morning and helped the princess with anything she needed throughout the day. It was enjoyable because she was my best friend, and it was nice to get to spend every day with her. After getting Emmie ready, we would go to the community gardens where we would spend our days learning about flowers, herbs, vegetables, and fruits. Everything we needed to feed and take care of our society.

Then, we'd go back home where I would tend to her before spending time with my mother, who was teaching me the art of making elixirs—also meant to help our people, especially now that the sun had become unreliable.

Most believed this was all happening because of the crystals. They said Aurora had abandoned us. Some believed there was nothing we could do and that the end of the world was near, but I disagreed. I refused to lose hope.

So, each time another crop died from the black sickness spreading through our land, I decided that instead of wallowing, I would focus on figuring out how to save us.

And the only way I knew how to do that was by honing my skills as a healer. Skills I was gaining from my mother.

To others, she was a savior, as she'd healed many through the years. She was the healer revered by all and now I was poised to inherit her status and her knowledge, as long as I didn't stray from the path laid out for me.

In reality, I wanted more. I wanted better. I didn't want to just follow in my mother's footsteps; no, I wanted to forge my own path and leave my own mark.

However, I knew nothing beyond this world. Beyond the castle I'd been born and raised in. The castle where I'd most likely take my last breath.

A brilliant flash of white light stopped us in our tracks. The guards unsheathed their swords as the light grew, and a massive circle of energy pulled at my skin.

Beckoning.

I became transfixed by it. Why, I didn't know. Perhaps, because our world had been blanketed by so much gray I'd forgotten the meaning of light. The joy and the hope that came with it were foreign concepts once held as standard in Frentani.

I squinted as something darker took shape. A shadow in the light.

Ominous, intriguing, and terrifying.

The bigger the shadow grew, the more my heart seized with fear, as I realized this was not the kind of light that brought joy.

The shadow got closer, gradually taking shape.

Head, shoulders, torso, arms, hips, legs.

A straight back. A confident walk. A boastfulness I'd never seen before.

I clutched Emmaline's hand, pulling her away from the light and the shadow. The guards stood shoulder to shoulder, ready to face whoever had infiltrated our world.

"Emmie, let's go." My tone was urgent; the hairs on my body rising with hypervigilance.

"But what about my guards?" she squeaked, gentle as ever.

If the world ended, Emmaline would be the first to go. She didn't have a fighting bone in her body.

But she had me.

"They can defend themselves. We need to go. Now!" I yelled, trotting backward, unwilling to take my eyes off the figure emerging from the brilliant light.

The figure was a male—with inky black hair falling around his shoulders, skin pale and features refined yet masculine. His attire was black too, and unlike anything I'd ever seen. Strong hands toyed with what looked like a pocket watch, its chain hanging from his fancy coat. Something that looked like a skinny cravat was tied around his thickly corded neck muscles.

He stopped, surrounded by the guards. With a sneer on his full lips, he revealed perfect teeth as his gaze landed on us. I clutched Emmie tighter to me, my heart hammering with terror as streams of black smoke shot out of his palms and fingertips.

A fucking Demon.

My temple throbbed, hands sweating as I watched the tendrils of blackness swoop into the guards' chests, lifting them off the floor as if they were meat on hooks about to be butchered. All four guards let out guttural screams as they writhed in the air.

I pulled my best friend into me, wrapping my other arm around her waist. The guards' screams abruptly stopped and they crumpled to the floor while the male stood in the center like a god.

I knew what this was. I didn't know exactly who he was, but I knew what he wanted. He wanted to take my Emmaline.

Over my dead body.

Pivoting on one foot, I spun us around. "Run, Emmie."

She heeded my plea, and we took off, our sandals pounding on the cobblestone road.

Terror rushed through me as I heard his heavy footsteps approach.

"Faster, run faster!"

But it was too late. I turned in time as the Demon rushed forward with incredible speed, catching Emmie by the hair and yanking hard. She screamed in agony, an ear-piercing sound which cut my heart in half.

I gripped her even harder, knowing I'd leave a bruise, but refusing to let go of my best friend. Twisting myself, I kicked the asshole in the shin. He let out a throaty chuckle full of malice.

"Let her go!" My voice came out as a tortured demand as I continued to pull her away from the evil male.

He bared his teeth before letting out a dry laugh, lifted his free hand, and a streak of shadow burst through his index finger, which he pointed at me.

It swirled and danced in the air, inching closer to me, and yet, I couldn't move. It was as if he was hypnotizing me with his power.

"You have to run!" Emmie's sobs jumpstarted my mystified brain, my eyes growing wide as the shadow hovered mere inches from my face.

I considered following my friend's suggestion and running for my life, but there was no life in which I'd abandon her. Not only because I'd sworn an oath to always put the princess before myself but because I knew that if I let her go with this monster, I would never see her again. And this thought was more terrifying than facing the evils this Demon was sure to dish out.

So, instead of fleeing, I rooted my feet to the ground, my hold on Emmie's waist tightening as I locked eyes with the Demon, challenging. Beckoning him to do his best, or rather, his worst.

The curl of his lips told me he accepted my challenge. Then, with a subtle flick of his hand, the shadow wrapped around my neck with such force, I lost my footing and my hold on Emmie.

My breathing grew ragged as the Demon's shadow magic squeezed, causing the veins in my neck to tighten.

Looking up, I found the male's gaze fixed on me, dark and threatening. The edges of my vision blurred as my struggle for breath intensified.

Emmie's cries never ceased, but they didn't deter him from continuing to grip her by the hair.

My whole life replayed in my mind as it became clear I was about to die.

My limbs became languid as my life force seeped out. I wanted to close my eyes and surrender to my fate, but I told myself never to give up. If not for me, then for my friend.

With the strength I had left, I looked at my friend. "I love you," I croaked. Emmie's cheeks were rivers of despair I wouldn't be able to dry.

"For fuck's sake," the Demon muttered.

He released me, and I fell to my knees as the shadow retreated back into his finger. I coughed, struggling for breath.

I willed myself to recover, afraid of what he'd do next. I couldn't afford to lose sharpness of my senses.

His arm wrapped around her waist, while he covered her mouth and muffled her cries. She thrashed in his hold, but he didn't move an inch.

While I was taller and stronger than the average female, Emmie was frail and petite, her heart too kind to face off against pure evil.

I lunged at him, punching him in the throat with a deftness I didn't know I had in me. He staggered back, coughing, but never letting go of the princess.

I didn't know males like him existed. Tall, strong, and mean. Nothing like the boys in Frentani.

"You let her go this instant!"!" I yelled. This time, he didn't laugh. This time, he looked angry.

"You shall pay for that." Despite his composed demeanor, the inflection in his voice hinted at the unfathomable torment waiting for me.

Still, I refused to give up. "You can't take her."

"Says who? You?"

"Yeah, me." I got in his face, fists resting on my hips, doing my best to appear confident and unafraid despite the fact that my legs were shaking. "You'll take her over my dead body."

The bastard chuckled. Emmaline was still thrashing in his grasp, sobbing and helpless.

"Killing insignificant vermin like you is below my purview," he said, before hooking his fingers on my golden belt. "But don't worry, after you see what awaits you, you'd wish you were dead." With that, he pulled me to him with ease, as if I were just an Angel's feather.

Panic rose in me as his words sunk in. He'd promised torture and misery. And the evil bastard had called me vermin. I was positively offended.

But my fear and indignation were squashed as a flutter sounded behind him. I craned my neck to find leathery black wings, bony and shiny, with two large talons protruding from them.

Shit. Definitely a Demon, and a powerful one at that.

My feet left the ground. Emmie's screams intensified. I kicked back, trying to hit him so he would drop us. Maybe I'd break an arm or a leg when I hit the ground, a possibility far better than being kidnapped and abused by a Demon.

I kept my voice steady for my friend's sake, though I couldn't deny I wanted to scream and cry as she was, but I couldn't afford to lose my head. We couldn't afford it.

"Emmaline, hold my hand." She took it, while the shadow Demon continued to flap his wings, pulling us up, up, farther and farther from the ground until we were so high above, I could see the city of Vestini sprawled out.

The only home I'd ever known.

The wind pelted my eyes. I wanted to close them, but the silhouette of the castle in the distance kept my attention. The once luminous golden turrets looked dull against the cloudy sky. I could see the stretch of the gardens we'd just left, and the lanterns down every street flickering on and off, failing us like the sun had failed us. Like the guards had failed us. Like the people cowering down below had failed us. Like I'd failed my best friend.

Because once he flew us into the light, our world forever changed.

BEETAH

A JOLT OF PAIN COURSED THROUGH MY VEINS. The feeling of swallowing sand sat in my throat. My stomach growled. I moaned, moving to my hands and knees as I shook my head from side to side, only to regret it when more pain hit my temples, radiating all over my skull.

I tried hard to open my eyes, but my lids felt like dead weight. Heavy and stiff.

"Get up."

And then it all came flooding back. The male. The Demon. The ominous shadow in the white light.

The face and the dark hair and the spellbinding green eyes.

The princess. The princess!

"The prin… prince…" I struggled to get the word out. Everything hurt, and hopping into that portal had not only knocked me out but it had given me a serious case of nausea. I swallowed down the urge to vomit. "Eh—Emmaline."

"Shut up." A growl.

"Where's the princess?" I said, forcing my lids to open. Inch by inch, they did, and what greeted me was darkness.

A darkness like I'd never seen before. I lived in the land where the sun always lit our way, its rays seeping through every recess. Wherever we were, there was no sun, and this notion terrified me more than anything. I scanned the room, noting the lack of windows. No wonder there was no sunlight.

Then came the scent. Musty and old. Then came touch; the feel of cold irregular stone under my palms and fingertips. Something dampish and squishy and unnerving. I crouched, unsure of what I'd touched, trying to look around, but all I saw was darkness. Except for the dim light of a torch right next to a pair of bright green eyes staring down at me.

"Who are you?" I croaked, a flash of anger rolling through me when I sounded the opposite of strong, confident, or fierce. But my body felt like a broken vase haphazardly glued back together.

Everything hurt.

"Who are you?" I repeated in a firm voice.

He chuckled, the sound rumbling through me, causing me to shiver. Despite the low lighting, I could see he had broad shoulders.

Thick, corded arms crossed over his chest, as he stared down at me with nothing in his gaze. Vacant. Hollow. Barren of any emotion besides boredom. "You're only here because your loyalty to your mortal princess made it hard for me to kill you like I killed her puny guards."

I thought the cretin didn't bother with "vermin" like me. Anger bubbled inside. Also, He was so infuriatingly handsome, I wanted to spit in his face.

I was glad I'd fought for us. I steeled my back, unwilling to show any more weakness to this asshole, despite being in excruciating pain.

"I wouldn't tell anyone else about this. Wouldn't want everyone to know a female half your size bested you," I blurted, unable to remain silent.

Keep your mouth shut, Reetah.

I wanted to wince at my stupidity. If he decided to kill me faster than intended, I only had myself to blame. But it wasn't in my nature to lie down and take it.

Heat burned across his features, gaze hardening even more. I braced myself for a slap or a stab from the dagger resting on his leather-clad hip. Or maybe he'd hurt me with the weird contraption hanging from his belt. It was shaped strangely with a short barrel and a handle which seemed to be filled with a shimmering blue liquid.

I knew what the liquid was. I'd learned about it through the history books from the castle library. The substance wasn't quite liquid but it also wasn't solid. It was the magical essence which powered another realm in our world.

Raetia.

The object the Demon possessed was called a pistol, supposedly capable of shooting people dead, piercing through skin and organ just like an arrow would.

Why did he have one of these things? My mind ran amok with possibilities. Perhaps it had been a gift or maybe he stole it. But then I remembered he'd come through a portal, and he was dressed strangely, which meant he wasn't from Frentani. No, the bastard was from another realm entirely, and since he hopped through a portal to get to this repugnant dungeon, I could only assume we were far from home.

My fear was so profound my limbs went numb, my gut telling me we were in Raetia. If my suspicions were correct, Emmaline and I were in a world of trouble.

Raetia was famous for being the most ruthless and advanced of the five realms in our world. Their aether magic allowed them to create many things which were unheard of in my realm or any other, for that matter. Raetians were famous for their advanced transportation and communication devices. They also were pioneers when it came to weapons, which meant their military was the biggest and most revered.

My mouth went dry and that primitive part of my brain wanted nothing more than to flee. But I needed to find Emmie.

The Demon's nostrils flared, his sharp jaw ticking with what looked like anger. But instead of punishing me for my big mouth, he huffed, turning toward the ornate iron door, torch in hand. The door slammed behind him, and I was engulfed in complete and utter darkness.

BEETAH

Y EYES SNAPPED OPEN.

The awareness of where I lay made my soul sink. The musty, cold dungeon cell was wrapping its tentacles around me, encircling me in darkness.

I couldn't remember when I'd fallen asleep or for how long, and the lack of windows or light didn't help. I was disoriented, and it was unnerving.

Tendrils of dread tugged at my heart, making me feel hopeless.

But hopelessness was my enemy, as it could keep me from wanting to fight, which simply wasn't an option.

I sighed. My skin felt sticky, my hair matted, and my feet were wet from the moss.

And then I remembered the shadow Demon and the way he'd looked at me, like he wanted to kill me for defying him. Why he didn't was beyond me.

Oh, right, he thought I was beneath him. And seeing as how I was just a mere mortal, I probably was, but that didn't mean I'd make his agenda easy for him to achieve.

Whatever torture he planned for me, I'd endure it with dignity.

He'd most likely intended to kill me at that moment. After all, he had no use for me. The Demon had only wanted Emmaline, but since I'd refused to let her go, he had no choice but to go through the portal with both of us in tow. And now I didn't even know where she was.

Was she in another cell? Somewhere down here in this dungeon? Or had she been taken elsewhere? If they abducted her, it was because they wanted her as a bargaining chip against her father. And considering she was the princess of Frentani, they wouldn't kill her.

However, avoiding death might be a more dreadful fate than being buried. They could violate her in the most heinous way, and who knew what other atrocities they were capable of.

I let out a strangled sob. I wasn't a crier, but I'd never been in this situation before. Ambushed, assaulted, kidnapped, and kept captive with no clue to what lay ahead for me or Emmie. She was my best friend. More than that. She was my sister, and I couldn't stand the lack of control. The not knowing what was happening to her.

I took a shuddering breath, determined to find my strength. I had to make them value me enough not to kill me. Then I could find her and get us both out.

My body shivered with a level of cold I'd never felt before. We never really felt it in our realm because the sun was always out. Lately, we'd experienced it more, but nothing like this. Frozen to the bone. I didn't think I liked this stupid realm.

I stood, slowly spinning in place, closing and opening my eyes in hopes of getting used to the darkness.

I could see better, but not by much. I could tell where the bar door was, so I walked up to it and tried to peek into the corridor. Nothing. Silence. Bleakness. Desolation.

"Hello. Is there anyone there?"

I let out a ragged breath when I was met with more silence. Sliding my arms through the bars, I leaned forward, attempting to peek into the dimly lit hallway.

Frustrated with my limited vision, I sat on the dirt floor, the scent of soil permeating my nose. My stomach growled, and I hurt everywhere.

I didn't know how long I remained still.

Suddenly, despite the chill in the room and in my bones, heat bloomed deep in my belly. It was a pleasant sensation, and I welcomed it, hoping it wasn't some kind of fever which would make our escape more difficult. My eyes shut; I felt the warmth spreading from my abdomen to my extremities. When my eyelids peeled open, I gasped at the newfound clarity in my sight. It was odd, but I could perceive my surroundings with remarkable detail.

The stone walls had chips, cracks, and moss climbing up them. The dirt floor was patchy, dark, and green. I could see my hands and my dress, which was all but ruined. The clarity imbued my spirit with renewed determination. I needed to find my best friend.

Making my way back to the door, I called out once more, "Can anyone hear me?"

I didn't dare breathe for fear of missing a sound, anything that indicated I wasn't here all alone.

"Hello." A small croak, so faint I wasn't sure how I'd been able to hear it. But I knew who it was.

"Emmie!" My heart lurched in my chest, blooming with renewed hope.

"Ree?" Her voice was barely a squeak, laced with the type of fear which was a novelty to us both.

Closing my eyes, I gripped the bars of the cell gate so tightly my knuckles turned white. I tried to train my ear, tried to focus enough to figure out where her voice was coming from.

"Where are you?"

A whimper, a quiet wail, a sniffle. "Ree?"

I didn't answer but instead focused on pinpointing her location. She was so close.

"Ree?"

I felt my ears perk up in an unfamiliar way. As if I could detect the vibration of her voice and follow its path straight to her.

She was in the cell next to mine. I turned and quickly made my way toward the eastern stone wall of my small cell. I placed my hands on it, grimacing at the feel of moss. Something crawled over my pinky.

Gross.

Fisting a hand, I rapped on the wall. "Emmie, can you hear me?" I said, putting my ear close to the wall.

A shudder ran through me as I detected the soft pattering of legs and the gentle flapping of wings. I prayed to the Goddess no creepy crawlies would decide to take a tour of my ear canal.

A muffled knock came from the other side. Yes! I smiled, relieved to have her so close. "Reetah?"

"Yes, Emmie, I'm here. There's only a wall between us."

"Thank the Goddess you're here!" I could hear the desperation in her voice, and it weighed heavily on my heart.

"I'm going to get us out of here, you just need to hold on and be strong. I promise you."

"I know." Her tone sounded utterly defeated. I loved my friend more than anything, but in this moment, I wished her fierceness matched her beauty. Emmaline had always been a delicate flower. Beautiful, tender, kind, lovable, and loving. She'd never had to struggle. She'd never had to fight to protect herself. And her father had never cared enough to teach her how to wield a sword or even fight with her fists if need be.

My father had raised me to be strong and independent, teaching me the way of the sword from a young age.

I'd tried to convince Emmie to train with me, to learn to wield a sword or a dagger, or maybe a bow, but her father had refused, training her instead in the laws and royal aspects of ruling, since she was the only heir to the throne.

I bet he now regretted his choice.

"Are you still there?" Her voice was steadier which made me smile.

My hands began to roam over the wall. I needed to find a way to get to her. Digging my fingernails into the moss, I began to rip it off, feeling the resistance of the intricate layout of roots holding it in place. I ripped and ripped until the stone was bare.

My heart picked up when I realized the wall wasn't built with large slabs of stone but with brick. I pushed two fingers into one of them but it didn't budge.

"Emmie, I need you to push at the bricks in the wall."

"They're covered in moss and there's water trickling down the wall from the ceiling."

That explained the squishy moss. "Rip off the moss and start pushing on the bricks. This place smells ancient so I'm sure at least one of them will be loose."

My friend remained silent but I could hear the dull sound of ripping moss. It sounded like our childhood, when Emmie and I would tear our skirts to shreds climbing every tree around the castle grounds, to the dismay of our mothers.

The friction of rock on rock pulled me out of my memories. I ran a hand over the wall, stopping when stone moved beneath my palm. "Yes! Keep pushing on it, Emmie."

"Okay."

The brick in question was at knee level so I lowered myself to the ground and pushed on it. After a few shoves back and forth, the brick loosened enough to pull out. I placed it on the floor next to me. The hole it left behind was big enough for my hand and I wasted no time sliding it through to the other side.

My heart warmed when I felt Emmie's petite hand slip into mine. She was cold but alive and that's all that mattered.

Neither of us spoke for a while. We simply held each other the only way we could, and I hoped that my touch brought her comfort the same way hers did for me. "Emmie, can you kneel and peek through the hole?"

"Yes."

Letting go of her hand, I got on my knees and brought my face to the gap in the wall. My lips curled when a pair of pale blue eyes came into view but it vanished when I spotted the fat tears running down her pale cheeks.

"Emmie, dry your tears and listen to me. We're in a dungeon, in some kind of cell, and I don't think we're in Frentani."

"What?"

My heart squeezed as I watched the terror enter her watery gaze.

"Listen to me. There are no guards in the corridors, so we need to figure out how to get one of us into the other one's cell. I thought about knocking enough bricks out of the wall for you to crawl through but I'm sure the asshole Demon will spot it right away. Our only option is to dig a small tunnel under the wall."

"Why are there no guards?"

I pursed my lips, shaking my head. "I have no idea why. All I know is that we need to get out."

"They'll kill us."

"Maybe, but we need to try."

"But if your hunch is correct, we're in another realm. How will we get back home?"

"I don't know yet, but I'm going to figure it out. Once I've bashed in his skull, we will run. Where to, I'm not sure, but what I do know is that any other place in this realm is probably better than staying here."

"I don't know if I can do it, Ree."

"Yes, you can. Your life depends on it. My life depends on it because there's no way in hell that I'll ever leave you behind. If you go down, I go down with you. If you die, I die. Do you understand?"

She let out a soft whimper, followed by a deep sigh. I knew she was mulling it over. I knew she was trying to calm her emotions long enough to focus on what we needed to do.

By the Goddess, we would find a way out of here, and if there were others rotting in cages in this terrible place, cursed to the same fate, we would get them out too.

"It will take us a while to dig, and if he comes, he'll see it."

"Do you still have your cloak?"

"Yes."

"Whenever we're not digging, we'll cover the hole with our cloaks, make it look like we've been lying on them."

This had to work and we couldn't get caught or else the punishment would be severe. I didn't doubt it for a second.

"We can devise a plan to fight our way out of here."

"You know I don't know how to fight, Ree."

"Emmaline, I cherish you more than you'll ever know. I need you to trust me when I tell you that right now, you must be strong. Once we're in the same cell, I'll teach you some self-defense. We're not playing around in the garden, reading books, and painting anymore. Now, we become tough fighters, got it?"

"Yes. We shall become fierce females."

"All right. Good girl. Now, let's dig."

Y FINGERS ACHED.

Dirt was caked all over my hands, forearms, and under my fingernails. Emmie and I had barely spoken for the last several hours as we focused on getting to each other as fast as possible.

Thankfully, the water trickling down the wall kept the soil soft and easy to pull out. We were so close to finding each other's hands through the hole. I could feel it.

"Emmie, don't stop digging no matter what."

I clawed at the soil with desperation, ignoring the snapping of fingernails on rock and the Goddess-awful smell permeating the space.

I didn't know why the Demon had left us alone for so long, and a part of me yearned for food and water, but in this moment, I yearned to care for my friend more than anything else.

Caring for Emmie was all I knew, and though a part of me dreamed of bigger, unattainable things, I never once regretted the destiny set forth for me from the moment I was born.

Soon, I would also get to begin my journey as a healer, alongside my mother. I knew I'd never get to heal with magic, but the medicinal plants the Goddess gave us were magical in their own right.

The dirt beneath my hands glided away, and I gasped, perceiving it was Emmie who was pulling it out.

The next few minutes passed in a blur as I dug and dug, until I felt a muddy hand under mine.

"Reetah!" Her squeal delighted my ears, and when her muddy skirts came into view, I knew in my heart that we would be all right.

Once the hole was big enough for her petite frame, I took her by the hand and pulled her through. She tumbled atop me and we fell to the cold damp ground yet my heart had never felt so warm. I sat up and righted her.

My heart crashed when I took in the condition she was in. Her luscious blonde hair was matted, her face covered in dirt, her gold-speckled dress ripped and muddied. Black and blue surrounded one of her eyes, and it was swollen shut. I gulped to stifle a sob at seeing my wonderful friend in this state.

"I'm going to kill him," I hissed, my jaw clenching with the fury I felt.

Emmie brought a dirty hand to her face, wincing when her fingers met the bruise surrounding her eye. "One of his guards did it."

"Then, I'll have to kill them all."

She smiled up at me. "You've never killed anyone, Ree. What makes you think you can do it now?"

"Our lives were never in danger before, now they are, and I refuse to sit idle and let them abuse us."

"I bet father is regretting not allowing me to learn to wield a sword."

I grinned, nodding. "I thought the same thing."

Emmie scooted back, reclining on the wall. I followed suit.

"I should have trained with you even if he didn't approve."

"Yes, you should have, but it's too late for regret. All we can do now is deal with the present."

She nodded. Her stomach growled. Mine responded. "Do you think they'll feed us?"

Emmie shrugged. "Who knows. I don't even understand why we're here."

"My guess is they took you as a bargaining chip, though I'm not sure what they plan on bargaining for or what they'll do with us."

"Ree?"

"Hmm?"

"How can you see my mangled face in this darkness?"

The question shocked me as I'd assumed her vision would have also adjusted by now. "I'm not sure."

"I can't see you at all. Did they hurt you as well?"

"No, but they will. Unless we manage to get out of here before then."

She rested her head on my shoulder and I wrapped an arm around back.

"I'm scared, Ree."

"Me, too, Emmie."

We held each other for a long time, my heart clenching each time her body shook with what I knew were silent sobs. My tears burned down my cheeks, desolation trying to force its way in, but I couldn't let it. If I did, I doubted our survival.

"Did they…did they touch you?" It was the question which had been on my mind since I'd woken in this Goddess forsaken dungeon. The question I was most afraid to ask.

I didn't comprehend I'd stopped breathing until I felt her head shake against my shoulder. I let out a loud sigh. "Thank the Goddess."

"You?" she croaked.

"They haven't put a finger on me since we got here."

Her relief was palpable in the darkness. A few minutes later, I felt her breathing even out, and I knew she was asleep. Which meant I had to stay awake just in case someone came.

My eyes shot open at the sound of heavy footsteps in the distance. Emmie's head lay limp on my shoulder. I shook her. "Emmie, wake up!"

She jolted awake, and we sprung to our feet. "You need to crawl back to your cell and cover the hole with your cloak. Don't let them see your hands."

She nodded and got on her hands and knees. I unclasped my cloak. "I love you, Emmie."

"I love you, too."

She made quick work of getting to the other side. I covered the hole as the footsteps grew louder. Lying on the edge of the cloak, I closed my eyes and feigned sleep, doing my best to calm my breathing. He was a powerful Demon, which meant he had enhanced senses and could pick up on ragged breaths and erratic heartbeats.

The clanging of metal against metal pricked my ears. I was sure it was coming from Emmie's cell. I strained my hearing, trying to pick up on anything I could.

"Get up."

My body shuddered at the sound of his deep voice. I could hear the swishing of Emmaline's skirts as she stood. I stopped breathing when I picked up on what sounded like a heartbeat.

Buh-bum.

Buh-bum.

Then, another heartbeat, this one faster and more erratic.

Buh-buh-bum, buh-buh-bum.

I frowned confused, unable to understand how and why my sense of hearing had become so keen. I looked around the space, catching every shadow, crack and cranny, which reminded me my sense of sight also seemed more efficient than ever before.

What was happening to me?

"I want to go home." Emmie's voice was shrill with terror. Fisting my skirt, I breathed deeply through my nostrils, fighting the urge to crawl through our little tunnel and rescue her.

"What you want or don't want isn't my problem. Now, eat and drink. The boss doesn't want you looking sickly."

The boss? So, he wasn't the boss? I suppressed another shutter. More unknowns to contend with.

The clatter of what sounded like a metal tray startled me. At least they were feeding us.

He shut Emmie's door. His feet resumed their pounding. He was getting closer. I stood, careful to keep my cloak covering the hole. Wiping my soiled hands on the back of my skirt, I hoped he wouldn't spot the dirt and mud caked under my fingernails, giving away what I'd been up to in the last few hours.

The door opened, and the orange glow of a torch danced into the space, followed by the body carrying it. His heavy black boots, followed by strong legs and broad shoulders curtained by silky tresses. My eyes honed in on the smoothness of his skin. I could see each individual hair on his square jaw and upper lip. Every detail enhanced, down to the tiny orange flecks swimming in his emerald eyes, and the light freckle adorning a corner of his mouth.

"Are you done staring? I can have someone paint you a picture, if you'd prefer."

I swallowed hard, unaware of how long I'd stared for, and mortified he thought I was admiring him, rather than trying to grasp why I could see so well.

"I was simply imagining how good your head will look detached from your body."

His smirk brought out an otherworldly beauty which only made me hate him more. "And who, pray tell, will be doing the detaching?"

"Does it matter? As long as you die, I don't care who does it." Bloody hell, when would I learn to keep my mouth shut.

He approached me with a dangerous gait, but I refused to budge. The clench of his jaw accentuated the masculine sharpness of it, as he stared me down with those wicked green eyes. I jutted out my chest and stared back. The energy in the room thickened with animosity, terrifying and exhilarating all at once.

My newfound enhanced vision allowed me to take in every strand of hair, every slope and angle of his face. He was astonishingly beautiful. If he wasn't an evil Demon intent on hurting us, I might have been attracted to him.

After a few more moments of idle gazing, I rolled my eyes. "Whatever you came here to do, get on with it, I'm bored."

The fury in his eyes intensified, and I immediately regretted my words and attitude.

His hand shot out so fast I had no time to react. He fisted my hair and pulled me into him like I was a rag doll. I ground my teeth as my scalp raged, and my feet lost their place on the damp stone, greeting air instead.

"Let me go, you monster!" I writhed, hands grabbing at him, trying to pry his fingers off.

He brought me close to his face, and I shuddered when his hot breath stroked the shell of my ear. Fear pervaded my senses, though survival was more potent.

Without a second thought, I reared back before slamming my head down on his. Suppressing the excruciating pain triggered by my maneuver, I sprang into action as soon as he relinquished his grip on my hair.

Satisfaction surged through me when a sharp grunt escaped his throat, and I used the moment to pull out the dagger strapped to his hip before taking a few steps back until I hit the wall.

I heard his body hit the ground, hard. I'd knocked him out.

A maniacal grin spread across my face, drenched with fierce empowerment.

Take that, bastard.

Gripping the dagger in one fist, I ran to the open door, scanning the hallway to ensure no one else was there but all I found was a tray on the ground outside my cell, carrying a measly piece of what looked like old, hard-as-stone bread, and a cup of what I assumed was water.

Piece of shit bastard. The urge to bash in his skull and ensure he never woke up crossed my mind, but he was immortal and no longer a priority.

Running to the other side of the room, I pulled my cloak off the floor, making quick work of latching it around my neck. "Emmie, crawl through, now!"

Her hands appeared in no time as she made her way through our little tunnel. With my free hand, I pulled her to her feet. Without a moment to spare, we took off running.

This was it. There was no room for mistakes. Panic imbued my bones, but I ignored all of it, even the relentless throb in my head. The pain was worth it. I'd clocked him so hard he'd passed out.

He'd underestimated me, as everyone always did. The kind lady's maid from sunny Frentani couldn't be fierce, right? They were all so wrong about me.

Stepping out of the cell, we ran down a dark corridor. Strangely shaped lanterns lit the way. The light emanating from them—which seemed to come from some orb in the center—was blue rather than yellow, same as his weapon.

My heart constricted as I ran past one, two, three... countless bar gates lining up both sides of the corridor.

The hard squeeze Emmie gave me told me she was thinking the same. Perhaps we could save them. Perhaps this would be our only chance to do so. But truth was, I wasn't sure how long the Demon would take to wake up. We couldn't risk it.

At the end of the corridor was a set of stairs which we took two at a time, thanks to our penchant for staying active through our daily hikes around the castle grounds.

My body was athletic, and this was a blessing as I quickly reached the top landing and pushed on a tall, arched wooden door.

The moment I stepped over the threshold, light flooded me, a strange hum overwhelming my senses.

The first thing I noticed was the sky. A million stars glittered like diamonds against an inky backdrop, and a large white moon blazed like a beacon in the night sky. The brightness of the moon did nothing to dispel its mysterious and tenebrous mood, making it all the more eerie.

We were in an alleyway, the scent of must and decay hitting my nose. Though the space was dark, it was much brighter than the dungeon. The mouth of the alley was filled with light, and I could see bodies walking around in the distance. We made our way out of the dank space, my heart lunging toward my ribcage as I observed the scene before us.

A city.

The lampposts stood sentinel on cobblestone streets, akin to those from home, yet radiating a blue glow.

I raised my gaze to either side as an object unlike any I'd witnessed before darted past. A vehicle resembling an elongated cart propelled by metal pipes.

"By the Goddess," Emmaline breathed. Looking back, I saw her breath escape her lips, forming a visible cloud in the frigid air. It was shocking.

I spun in place, hands clammy and lungs frozen as I took in my surroundings. The towering buildings around me stretched ever upward, devoid of the greenery which covered every structure in Frentani. The jagged concrete designs were foreign to me, different from any city I'd seen before. The street teemed with people bustling to and fro. They were dressed in unfamiliar clothes made of dark colors, from black to grays and plums. Both men and women wore elaborate hats on their heads, tall and straight.

Emmie slipped her frigid hand in mine, and I tightened my grasp around it. We gripped each other tight, as we turned to gaze at the place we'd left behind.

Before us stood a behemoth of a mansion, ominous yet transcendent in its beauty. It was constructed from massive slabs of gray stone, with a wrought iron fence out front nestled into an ivy-draped wall that encircled the property.

The vines crawled up the walls like a parasite. The place was sealed off from the rest of the world, ancient and foreboding. A grand staircase led to a huge porch lined with ornate pillars whose paint had long since faded away, leaving behind only their monolithic cracked shells.

The mansion appeared to have three floors, each one stretching upward and breaking into pointy turrets that pierced the sky.

Ugly gargoyles looked down on us from their perch along the gutters, their grotesque cherubic faces twisted into malevolent snarls as they surveyed our small forms below. Their Demon-like features were both terrifying and fascinating, and I couldn't help but feel as if they were watching us with cold, calculating eyes; plotting our demise.

As we stood there, staring at this monumental structure before us, quiet whispers seemed to drift through the air like ghosts warning us of danger lurking within the place.

"We need to get out of here," I said, adrenaline coursing through me, warning me of the impending danger which I was sure would soon be waking and chasing after us.

"But, where do we go when we don't even know where we are or how this strange place operates?"

She had a point. Though I knew we were in Raetia based on the books I'd read and the general stories we'd all heard since childhood, we had no idea how to navigate this foreign land. I spun us, walking backward until we hit the fence surrounding the mansion, its vines caressing our backs and shoulders. I pressed my body into the vines, hoping it would be enough to shelter us from the evil walking inside the house.

Scanning the street before us, I watched as something that looked like a stagecoach stopped in front of the building, right by an iron bench, a lone ornate lamppost keeping it company, its lantern's glow blue just like the Demon's weapon. It seemed that just as everything in our realm was powered by the sun, aether powered everything here. I couldn't help but feel awed by everything around me—the abundance of aether-infused energy that seemed to power every object, the strange lights, and the mystery that seemed to fill the air.

A group of people exited the vehicle, which was clad in black but also gleamed with gold. A silver disc was securely attached to the man's arm with a black leather band, nestled against his skin like two pieces of a puzzle. The surface shimmered and glinted in the light, its reflective sheen looking almost like a pocket watch.

The grand carriage sped away and left no one behind to pull it, because it ran off its own rails, powered by some strange combination of metal and magic. Its wheels did not spin on dirt or grass, but glided over polished steel, as if it was air and earth bound at once.

My breathing was going haywire, along with my heart.

Because one thing was clear. This wasn't our world.

5

"**B**LOODY HELL," I GROUND OUT, holding my head with both hands as pain pulsated through my skull.

I looked around, disoriented, until it all trickled back into my memory.

The gate of the dungeon cell was wide open, though there was no little creature to be seen.

I didn't know her name. The girl with the luscious blonde hair. Squeezing my palm into a fist, I remembered the way the thick shiny strands felt in my grasp, and I suddenly wished to do more of it, preferably with my dick in the mix. Her plump tits looked snug in the gold-toned bustier covering her delectable hourglass figure. She was tall, fit, and could pack a punch. Or rather, a headbutt.

Few had the capability of knocking me out, but then again, few had ever tried. Apparently, she either didn't know who I was or had a death wish. I'd done a good job of building my reputation.

Demon. Bastard. Villain.

The little creature had caught me by surprise, and it would be the first and last time she ever bested me.

Letting out another pained groan, I stood, shaking my head to dispel the dizziness. I grabbed for the aether pistol on my hip, pulling it out and making my way down the dungeon's corridor. My cousin, Ruslan, and a couple of guards were walking toward me, with pistols in hand.

"What's going on?" Ruslan said. His keen eyes scanned me for injuries.

I shook my head again. Remnants of pain she'd caused refusing to leave me. "The fucking female that came with the princess escaped."

Ruslan threw his head back with laughter I didn't appreciate. I fisted a hand, ready to clock him in the jaw. Instead, I glared and sneered at him. This didn't stop his chuckle. "You let some little Frentanian female escape?"

I gripped my pistol so hard, growling in his face.

Yes, Ruslan was my best friend and cousin, but I wouldn't allow anyone to challenge my capabilities. Not even him. Especially when we were around our guards.

There was a reason my uncle had made me his right-hand man. His acquisitions officer trusted with the only crystals which could open portals to each of the realms in our world. I felt the crystals in question warm inside their pouch, which I always kept inside my jacket pocket.

Ruslan flinched at the sight of my forehead. "Nice knot you've got there," he said uneasily.

She'd smacked me hard enough to cause a bump.

Shoving past the men in front of me, I made my way to the stairs leading out of the hall. "Quit gawking and help me catch her, asshole."

Ruslan snickered, matching my pace and slapping a hand on my shoulder, making my brain rattle in my skull.

Rage surged through my veins and my hands itched to wrap around her neck and squeeze until the air left her lungs, never to be filled again.

Her slender, appetizing neck.

I'd grown up in this world. A world of darkness. A world which loved taking precious things filled with light and breaking them until they ceased to exist as they once were. Meanness was all I knew. But in those quiet moments of solitude, between dreaming and reality, I could feel the goodness buried deep inside of me, a goodness I was sure had been left there by the person I never knew but loved most in this world.

But even her love wasn't enough to wipe the badness invading the chasm where my heart should be. And when reality pulled me out of my dreams, her absence turned me into an even bigger monster, driving me to hate everything I was and everything I'd never be.

So, yes, I would find her, and when I did, I would use and abuse her to my heart's content.

Because she was worthless, just like her beloved princess.

Just like me.

I couldn't touch the princess, but nobody said I couldn't touch her. So I'd make her my plaything. After all, every female in Raetia bored me. They were snobbish and insufferable.

The prospect of tasting a female from a different realm was quite appealing.

I'd kidnapped countless Mystics but had never partaken in their taming, and I'd certainly never cared to tame a mortal.

But there was something about this creature that aroused the most primitive parts of me, the parts wanting to drown out the goodness buried deep within me. Worst of all, the little creature looked like her.

I knew because of the painting my father so proudly displayed in his study, as if he wasn't the reason why I'd grown up without my mother.

My jaw clenched so hard it intensified the sharp pain in my head. The pain she'd left there.

Her similarities to the one I'd yearned for most only served to anger me more.

Yes. I would use her until she no longer interested me. I would turn her into the best sex slave the Villa had ever had.

But first, I had to find her. Lucky for me, my sense of smell was unmatched and so was my memory.

Her scent would stay with me forever. All I had to do was follow it.

CHEETAH

As Emmaline and I made our way down the street, I took it all in.

The sights, lights, and smells were overwhelming. People's stares were disconcerting. I couldn't imagine what we looked like to them, dressed in clothing so different from their own, covered in mud, our wild and matted hair, and red-rimmed eyes that told of both exhaustion and heartbreak.

I wanted to shrink away from their judgmental gazes, yet at the same time I couldn't help but wonder what we looked like to them. Their judgmental stares called to mind hungry wolves regarding fresh meat: are we worth their time? They watched us pass and turned away without a backward glance.

And then, there was the night sky, or at least that was what I thought they called it. Gratitude for my mother filled me, for if she hadn't taken the time to teach me all she knew about the realms, we wouldn't have a fighting chance. Not that we had much of one anyway, but at least we knew where we were.

"Why did the Goddess make our realms so different from each other?" Emmie's voice penetrated my thoughts, and I turned to look at her. Despite the wretched state we were in, she looked as beautiful as ever.

"I don't know why, Emmie, but she must have had her reasons."

Spotting an alley wedged between a bakery and what looked like a place that sold jewels, I pulled us both toward it. Once we were concealed, I peeked back to where we came from, making sure the Demon wasn't following us.

I breathed a sigh of relief when I saw no one I recognized. The streets were crowded, despite the chill in the night air. Obviously, these people were in their element while Emmie and me were not.

Far from it.

"Do you see him?"

I looked back at my best friend. "No, but that doesn't mean we should linger."

"How could we not linger when we have nowhere to go?"

Pursing my lips, I stared out at the street, pondering our next move. My friend was right, this realm was quite different from ours, and figuring out how to find our way in such an unfamiliar world was daunting.

The Aurora was our creator, the one most thought of as a Goddess. Though there were quite a few who believed it to be a genderless energy. The Aurora created the Island of Anathema, which housed the mythical crystal forest powering our world. Each crystal within the forest carried a different life force assigned to supply the energy to bring life into existence. There were crystals assigned to each of the four realms surrounding the Island of Anathema: Frentani, Lucania, Volsci, and Raetia.

Based on the blueish lights inside the homes and on the lampposts, as well as the fashion of those around us, I knew this was Raetia. Though the buildings and landscape of the city were similar to ours, they also couldn't be more different.

The cobblestone streets had rails running through the center for powered wagons. A floating railroad lay above the city, another strange type of wagon—though much faster—running on it.

Luscious vines didn't cover the walls of every home and building. Their roofs didn't have trees jutting up toward the sky. While people in my realm wore light and sheer fabrics in yellows, whites, and golds, the people here donned thick fabrics in dark colors, and lots of leather, sexy skirts with thigh splits or rolled up in the front, while the back hung down to the ankles. There were no flat shoes or sandals in sight. Instead, every woman wore elegant boots with high heels and lace details, while the men wore shiny and masculine ones.

Elaborate leather pouches hung from waists by expensive buckles.

Men donned fancy suits in dark colors with a thin piece of fabric tied around their necks like a skinny cravat. Their coats were shorter in front and longer in the back.

And no one walked around barefoot, though I couldn't blame them because the weather here was colder. And aether powered everything.

Aurora didn't give aether to my realm. She gave us the sun and then, in place of aether, she gave us witches. All witches were native to Frentani. But over the last hundred years, more witches had been born without magical powers. The Stygian's corruption of the Crystal Forest took magic away from witches, thus bringing the earth witch.

Earth witch was a fancy way of calling a powerless witch who had to make-do with learning about herbs, and how to draw on the healing qualities of nature. We were also called healers, which I preferred because calling myself a witch of any kind felt unauthentic and misleading.

Yes, at the end of the day, that's what we were. Every female from my mother's bloodline should have been born a magical witch but instead we all lacked magic, and I wanted nothing more than to be the first of many generations to be blessed with such a gift. But I knew I'd never wield such abilities because my kind had been forgotten, abandoned, forsaken.

"We must keep going," I said, grabbing Emmie by the hand. Stepping out of the alley, we made our way down the street, my cheeks heating when a new wave of onlookers gawked in our direction.

So I stared back, shocked to find their hair ranged from black and brown to lavender, pink, and even green.

Curious.

My hands shook with adrenaline, but I kept walking briskly, never letting go of Emmie's hand, turning every so often to make sure the Demon wasn't giving chase.

We walked for so long my limbs also trembled. I halted my steps, my breathing heavy as I tried to ignore the onlookers. Emmie's chest crashed into my back and I turned, noticing her discomfort.

"They're all gawking at us," she whispered, a mess of matted blonde hair obscuring her bruised face.

It broke my heart to see her this way.

We needed to get back to our realm, or we'd be here for the rest of our lives. The thought sent a deep chill down my spine. To remain here was a terrifying possibility, without our families, lost in a world we knew nothing about.

We shuffled along the street, my arm supporting Emmie's wilting body. She glanced up at me with heavy eyes, and I felt a tug in my heart. With our stomachs growling, I desperately wished we had stopped to beg for a free meal from the bakers or eateries we passed.

It was clear to me that begging was now a part of our lives. I didn't see how else we could receive the sustenance we needed to survive. It occurred to me that perhaps we needed to get out of this city and find the countryside.

Perhaps we could chance upon a village, where the locals would display an open-minded attitude and eagerness to assist two wayward females.

Emmie, squeezed my hand, stopping in front of a shop displaying a beautiful outfit on the window. A dark gray leather bustier type garment and a long black skirt with a thigh split. It was so beautiful, in another life, I would have wanted to go inside and buy it.

"Maybe we can change our clothes and blend in better."

I frowned at her idea. "We have no money to buy anything, Emmie."

"I know, but look, there's a lady in there. Perhaps she would be kind enough to help us."

I pursued her glance to spot a gorgeous woman with lush emerald tresses and striking scarlet lips stationed at a counter.

Emmaline opened the door to the shop, a bell chiming above our heads.

The female we'd seen through the display window turned her head in our direction, her eyebrows rising as she scanned us from top to bottom. I didn't miss the flitting look of disgust that crossed her face right before she cleared her throat and straightened her spine. She approached us, resting her hands in front of her navel the way Emmie had been trained to do during special events.

I let the door shut behind me, my hands nervously running down my muddy skirt. I opened my mouth to speak but shut it when Emmie took the lead.

"Hello, I am Princess Emmaline of Frentani. This is my best friend, Reetah. We are in need of your assistance."

The shop attendant scoffed, her face a picture of incredulity as she sized us up, grimacing when she took in our matted hair. She fixated on our heads, her grimace shifting into awe and curiosity. "Your hair," she said, taking a few steps closer, "it's like spun gold. I've never seen anything like it."

"Just as we'd never seen green hair until now."

She looked at me, a calming smile on her lips. "How do I know you're telling the truth? That you're the princess, I mean."

"Our hair color and attire tell you where we are from but I cannot prove to you I'm the princess, all I can promise is that if you help us, my father will generously reward you."

The female looked astonished. "The Princess of Frentani," she muttered to herself, as if she still couldn't believe it.

Pride swelled in my chest at Emmie's confidence, taking the reins and using her title as a tool to get us out of this realm.

"Yes, that I am," said Emmie, smiling at the lady.

"By the aether, you look like you've gone through a terrible ordeal." She ushered us inside.

I scanned the shop, recognizing the beauty of the fashions she sold and yet unable to enjoy it. All I wanted was food, shelter, and a way back home.

She stopped in front of a large leather sofa. "My name is Kira. Now, please, have a seat and tell me, how did you get here?" The concern on her face was comforting. It felt as if we'd finally found an ally in this wretched place.

We both sat on the sofa while the female sat on an ornate chair in front of us.

"A Demon took us from our realm," I said, the quiver in my voice betraying my emotions. I was tired, afraid, heavy with the weight of the unknown. "We traveled through a portal and woke up in the dungeon of a mansion not far from here."

Something seemed to change in her expression, the kindness in her eyes ebbing for a split second before her mouth split into a warm smile. "I can't imagine what you've both gone through." She turned her gaze to the door of the shop. "Excuse me a moment, I'm going to lock up for the day and then we will get you cleaned up and fed."

Emmie and I returned her smile, melting into the comfortable sofa, though I couldn't ignore the tightness in my chest, the tingling sensation in the back of my mind telling me not all was as it seemed.

I watched her saunter to the door where she turned the lock before flipping a wooden sign hanging on the window from open to closed. Then, she made her way back to us but my eyes remained glued on the window display, admiring the outfit we'd spotted before coming in. The bustier had ribbons crisscrossing in the back and no sleeves. It was so different from our fashion in Frentani, I couldn't stop gawking at it.

"I see you like the ensemble I've put together," the female said. I turned, jolting at her proximity. She was so close to my face, her dark brown eyes hinting at something sinister before she once again plastered a grin on her face.

Unease prickled my skin. Something wasn't right.

"Perhaps you could help us with some fresh clothing to help us blend in?" Emmie said giving the shopkeeper that bright smile not many were able to resist.

There was a glint in the woman's eyes before she nodded. "Of course, it's the least I can do. Now, follow me and we'll have you looking brand new in no time."

She guided us to the back of the place and into a large room replete with rack after rack of all kinds of dresses, bustiers, and skirts. Boots lined the opposite wall. She sifted through one of them before pausing to look at us. "I think I have the perfect ensemble for you in the front of the shop, after all, you couldn't stop looking at it a minute ago." She gave us a polite nod. "The washroom is over there"—she pointed to a door in the back of the room—"why don't you both clean up while I go get your clothes."

Emmie and I both nodded in gratitude. She shut the door, leaving us alone.

"You can go clean up first, Ree," Emmie said.

I shook my head. "No, we go into the washroom together, I won't let you out of my sight."

Emmie gave me a tired smile before leading the way into the washroom. There was a large mirror on the wall. I cringed when I took in our appearance. No wonder everyone stared at us. That and the fact we had blonde hair, a characteristic unique to those from our realm.

The glide of the wet washcloth along the skin of my face felt incredible and I realized how many things I took for granted in my life. Things like cleanliness, food, and safety.

It all happened so fast. Me looking up at the mirror behind us, locking onto furious green eyes, watching as his gloved hand clamped over my mouth and most of my face.

Watching in helpless horror as another male did the same to Emmie.

I dropped the washcloth, my hands reaching up to pry his off my face. I couldn't breathe. The Demon gripped both my wrists in his free hand, clutching them against my chest and he dragged me out of the washroom. Emmie's screams were muffled against her captor's palm and I clenched my eyes shut. How did he find us?

I thrashed in his hold as a group of males surrounded us. All dressed in black. They smiled, like seeing a defenseless female in this monster's grasp gave them the utmost pleasure. The shopkeeper came back into the room but she didn't look at us, her eyes locked on one of the men. She walked up to him, and I watched in horror as he pulled her into him and kissed her. They moaned with their tongues dancing, displaying a complete lack of decorum.

I could feel my heart racing with fury. She'd tipped them off. Sun above, they were all monsters! At that moment, as I bucked and writhed to save myself from his clutches, I learned that a handsome face meant nothing. Evil came in all packages.

I pounded my fists on his thighs, to no avail. He was too big, too strong for the likes of me. I refused to give up and kept pounding into him.

He growled, "Stop hitting me."

I bit down on his finger, causing him to pull his hand from my mouth. "I won't stop until you let us go!"

The rumble of his amused chuckle vibrated through my spine, and I hated that it somehow thrilled me.

"Dream on, Little Creature."

"Don't call me that. I'm not some kind of animal."

"Could've fooled me with the way you're behaving."

"Why am I here?" I kept screaming, but he didn't answer. I could hear the others chuckle like this was a joke to them. There was nothing funny about this.

A maelstrom of fear, worry, and rage went through me. But defiance won.

Screw this piece of shit. The reason I was here was to protect the princess at all costs. I would figure out a way to get us out of this realm.

My hand went for his crotch. I fisted his bulge and squeezed as hard as I could, while stomping on his foot with all my might.

He groaned in agony, and the second he let me go so he could cup his balls and cry like the bitch he was; I took my chance. Scrambling backward, I pulled his dagger out of my girdle pouch. "Stay away from me," I panted, pointing the dagger in their direction. "You stay away from me or you'll regret it." I took a step back, trying to reach Emmaline who was still struggling against the other male's grasp.

Emmie managed to rip the Demon's hand off her mouth and screamed, "Run!"

I stared at her wide-eyed. I didn't know what to do. If I ran, I may manage to escape and then go back to the mansion to rescue her.

But what if I couldn't get in? It was clear trusting people around here would be next to impossible. I glared at the treacherous shopkeeper, Kira, her arms hung around the male's shoulders as she peppered kisses on his neck. Did people in this realm not attain to the rules of privacy?

Ugh.

"Run, please!"

Tears streaked down my best friend's face, the plea in her eyes tearing me in half. I didn't want to run, didn't want to leave her behind, but now that I knew where to find the dungeon she was sure to return to, I could rescue her. I had to rescue her.

I glared at the group of evil males as they all continued to laugh. I never imagined someone's myrrh could enrage me. Blood boiling, I backed up a few more paces, though I really wanted to rush them and slit their throats. "Walk away, now," I said as I pointed the dagger at each one.

I kept stepping backward through the shop until my back hit the door. Reaching around me, I felt for the lock, awkwardly unlatching. Then I turned the doorknob and stepped out onto the street. The little bell above the door rang like a bad omen. The concerto of gasps from passersby didn't feel any better.

The males followed, all of them sneering and laughing, except the asshole Demon, who bore his eyes into me, uncaring of the growing number of people staring.

"Help! These men have kidnapped us!" I made eye contact with a group of young males across the street. "What are you standing there for? Help us," I yelled through gritted teeth.

But no one moved a muscle.

My words fell on deaf ears as they all bowed their heads and continued on their way.

The men chuckled again. "We are the authority. They will not listen to you," the shadow Demon said as he stepped out from behind his minions.

Hopelessness tasted bitter on my tongue. How would we ever get out of this?

I stood on shaky legs, still pointing the dagger at them as the shadow Demon took a few steps forward. I turned and ran for my life. But within seconds, someone yanked me back by my hair before punching my temple so hard I saw stars.

A deep angry voice invaded my ears, eyes like emeralds stared at me, a flutter of blurry Demon wings sent a cooling breeze over me, and then I succumbed to darkness.

BEETAH

LOUD BANGING JOLTED ME AWAKE.

Darkness surrounded me but I was quick to adjust to it. Tears pricked the back of my eyes when I realized I was back in my cell, back in captivity, curled up on the floor, my back to that damned metal door. The reek of mold and must made me gag and my bones ached from the chill, though my head felt as if it had been cleaved in half.

The shadow Demon stood in front of me along with two guards I hadn't seen before. His eyes were full of murder, like he wanted to drive his blade through my neck. He pointed at my hands and barked out his order.

"Tie her hands behind her back."

My mind screamed no. Fear coiled around my throat and the air caught in my lungs. "What? why?"

"Do you really need to ask?"

The air around me felt like fire, suffocating my lungs until I could barely breathe. I felt burning hot and ready to blister his flesh.

Sweat beaded and trickled down my back. My hands became hot, hands fisting until my knuckles whitened and my nails dug into my palms. Every part of me wanted to scream at him but the words froze on my tongue. All I could do was shoot him a piercing glare.

He rolled his eyes as if I was an annoying child. "You have a propensity to escape and beat people up. I won't fall for that again."

The feisty part of me won, and my tongue unfroze, ready to battle him with words. "I only beat people after they've attacked me. You deserved it."

"Perhaps. But I will not give you another chance to try. I won't allow you to believe you're in control, because you're not." He looked up at the guard. "What are you waiting for, pick her up."

Trying to ignore the pain in my skull, I allowed them to lift me up, repulsed by their meaty hands pawing at my arms. The scent of stale ale emanating from the two males made my eyes water.

Instead, I focused back on the shadow Demon, smiling wickedly. "Feeling threatened by a female?"

His eyes never left mine, and I could feel the tension in the air as he clenched his jaw in frustration. Goddess, I enjoyed taunting him. His chuckle was dark and menacing. "You're no threat to anyone, most of all, me. You're a servant from Frentani, the most pathetic realm in our world, and you smell."

Despite my wish to take offense, his opinion of me was inconsequential, unless it helped me flee. Still, I was curious. I gave him the sweetest smile, my petulance out in full force. "Can you explain that further?" I turned to the two guards, who were binding my wrists behind my back with leather straps. This fucking realm and their leather. My smile morphed into a wince when one of them pulled me up by my hair, bowing his head to growl in my face with that abhorrent breath.

"Hey, asshole, is that really necessary?" I hissed, my jaw clenching from the searing pain on my scalp.

Pain disappeared, replaced by a blaring scream that slipped out of my throat as something whizzed above me. I felt a hot liquid splash across my face and looked on in shock as the guard's head detached from his body and rolled onto the floor with a sickening thud. His lifeless hand fell from my hair like a deadweight.

My heart pounded madly and my limbs trembled uncontrollably as I spun around to confront the shadow Demon who stood still, his sword shining in the firelight, blood dripping from its sharp edge.

Keeping his intense eyes on me, he removed a handkerchief from his pocket and calmly wiped away the blood from his blade, as if lopping off someone's head was an everyday occurrence for him. He cast a menacing glance at the other guard, who had gone pale with terror. "You treat her like that," he said icily, "and you will also bear the brunt of my wrath."

I stared at him, dumbfounded, and then threw my head back and laughed, partly from nerves and partly because he was the most ridiculous male I'd ever met. He was a villain who kidnapped me and put me in a dungeon. But now, he was indignant when his guard—whom he sent to restrain me—did it roughly?

The agony in my head was a testament to his physical assault, far graver than the guard's menacing whisper in my ear.

Goddess, he was infuriating.

When my laughter waned, I looked back over at him. He wasn't amused, but said nothing.

Fists on my hips, I cocked my head and stared him down. "You dare punch me hard enough to knock me out, but will kill another for less?" My nostrils flared, my eyes narrowing on his stupidly handsome face. "Sounds quite hypocritical, if you ask me."

"It's a good thing no one is asking for your opinion," he said coldly as he grabbed me by the back of the neck and pushed me out of the cell. Even with my wrists bound together, I still tried to resist.

The warmth of his breath fanned across my ear. "Let me make it clear that I didn't do the hitting, but the person who did breathes no longer."

As I gazed into his eyes, sincerity shined through, sending me further off balance. "Why would you do that?"

"Because I'm the only one who gets to touch you."

Oh.

Sun melt me.

Straightening my shoulders, I pretended his words didn't affect me. "You better be taking me to see Emmaline."

"Like I said, you're not in control."

He was such a prick.

"I'm not asking you again. Tell me where you're taking me."

I felt my skin crawl as his deep, throaty laughter echoed in the surrounding air. I hated the way my heart sped up at the sound of his voice and equally despised the intoxicating smell that lingered when he was near. He was a Demon, and he repulsed me—or so I thought. No matter how hard I tried to resist it, a part of me was inexplicably drawn to him, and this realization filled me with fear and confusion.

Turning my head, I looked behind me, trying to push him out of my mind. The guard who managed to remain alive followed closely, the rows of blue light glowing in the lanterns giving him an eerie glow. Cobwebs crept along the gray walls, tiny spiders quickly scurrying in and out of the cracks in the stone. My ears picked up on faint whimpers coming from the row of cells to my right. I took a quick look and noticed a group of women confined to a single room. They were clustered on the ground, their garments torn and soiled.

Sorrow. So much sorrow. It reached out to me like tentacles tugging at my legs, beckoning me to share in their desperation.

I could only make out a few of their faces, my heart plummeting when I discerned that Emmie wasn't with them.

Where was she?

I dedicated the rest of our walk down the ominous corridor to scrutinizing each cell, hoping to spot my best friend. But she wasn't there. The notion was unnerving to say the least. Perhaps it was for the best. After all, I couldn't shake the feeling I was walking toward my demise. I was a dead female walking.

When we approached the end of the corridor, I saw the exit we'd escaped through, but instead of heading that way, we turned right, making our way down another equally creepy hallway.

The Demon's steps halted in front of a set of large, wooden double doors, engraved with carvings of two beasts locked in an epic struggle. Their taut muscles and life-like movements depicted something I had only seen in books.

The guard opened one door for us to pass through, and we continued down an airy corridor wide enough to be a house. Each side was lined with doorways, but the place seemed deserted.

My eyes widened at the sight before me. The open hall resembled something out of an ancient castle or palace—Cathedral ceilings soared twenty feet up through detailed archways and ornate sculpted moldings encircling my vision everywhere I looked. Macabre paintings depicting Demons consuming children and women hung at the foot of a magnificent staircase adorned with intricate carvings on its banister.

I looked up at the large black crystal chandelier hovering above the top landing. Iridescent light danced across its surface, blinding me and setting my teeth on edge.

As I reached out to touch the figures, I felt a shiver run down my spine. They were cherubs with demonic expressions etched onto their faces, their eyes vacant and yet, it was as if they could see right through me. And though I wanted to turn away, I couldn't take my eyes off of them.

The scent of tobacco and cologne hung heavily in the air around us, mixed with a sickly-sweet perfume that made my nose twitch. We continued up and up, higher than I ever thought possible, each step filling me with an unsettling emotion. Why didn't I run the first time Emmie told me to run? I should have listened.

As we climbed, my conflicting thoughts began to consume me until all I could do was wonder what horrors awaited me at the top.

"What is this place?"

The dickhead ignored me, and the heat of his large hand pressing against my neck made my skin sweat. I stopped, planting my feet and wishing I could cross my arms. "I'm not walking until you tell me where we are," I growled.

He stared down at me, fury in his gaze. And heat. Like he enjoyed my resistance. "Very well." That's all he said before bending over, gripping the back of my knees, and swinging me over his shoulder. My stomach whooped, my heart skipped a beat, and, for some insane reason, a tingle coursed between my thighs.

"Put me down, asshole!"

Being unable to move my arms pissed me off, and I had no choice but to focus on keeping them glued behind my back so they wouldn't swing down and dislocate my shoulders.

A hard smack on my ass made me yelp in surprise, and I sucked in a breath. It didn't hurt, but it shocked me. "Keep quiet."

"Did you just spank me?"

"Yes, and I'll do it again unless you stay quiet, and this time, I'll make sure to remove every obstacle between your pretty little ass and my hand. Got it?"

"I hate you."

"Splendid."

Sun melt me, I wouldn't rest until I killed him.

We stopped in front of another door. "Wait here," he said to the guard as he crossed the threshold, shutting the door behind us. Lifting my head as much as I could, I took in the space. A plush burgundy carpet, a sitting area with a giant fireplace, and a four-poster, equally giant bed. I spotted large windows though they were obscured by thick green curtains.

My muscles tensed and my thoughts raced with a myriad of possibilities the instant he flung me onto the bed. Was he planning on beating me? Violating me?

I desperately wanted to scream or cry out, but something inside forced me to keep a calm facade, making eye contact with him as if nothing was wrong despite the fear coursing through my veins. Fear I was sure he could scent.

"A bath has been drawn for you." He pointed at a door on the far end of the bedroom. "Clean up."

"Um, I can't take my clothes off with my hands tied behind my back. I'm not magical. I'm not a bloody Angel or a Demon who could just think her clothes off."

He took out his dagger—the one I'd temporarily stolen—then walked around the bed until he was at my back. I tried to scurry away, but he put a heavy hand on my shoulder. "Don't move."

I froze as I felt him grip my bound wrists in his hand before he sliced through the leather.

"Only Angels can think their clothes off." He walked out, the sound of the lock clicking echoing through the empty room.

I was a prisoner.

I sat on the edge of the mattress, feeling my energy draining away. My tired eyes studied the room around me. Dark wooden dressers and wardrobes lined the walls, each of them built with masterful workmanship. The curtains were thick and soft, their green so dark it resembled pine trees.

As I ran my hands over one of the bedposts, I examined the carvings on the canopy and headboard; highly detailed images of a battle between monsters and dragons.

Why dragons? They weren't even part of this world, as they were native to Lucania, the land with perpetual moonlight. Everything about this place was strange and mysterious, but I was too exhausted to try and figure it all out.

It took me a while to move off the bed, but eventually I made my way to the bathroom, rubbing at the red angry marks around my wrists.

Steam wafted from the claw-foot tub, the warm water calling to me. I couldn't peel my filthy clothes fast enough. Dust and grime streaked my skin, sticking to it like rain on pavement. Every inch of my body felt dirty, from my hair to the soles of my feet.

A tall, imposing mirror stood in the corner, framed in ornate cast iron scroll work. Another exquisite piece of furniture in this prison of mine. I flocked to it, staring at the reflection of my naked body, bruised and battered, just like my soul.

I couldn't understand why he was granting something as pleasant as a bath when it was clear he couldn't care less about me.

My body melted the moment I stepped into the tub, the warm water soothing my aching muscles. Head and all, I submerged myself and let out a cathartic scream while watching bubbles escape my mouth and rush to the surface, the dull sound of my voice somehow bringing me comfort in this twisted situation.

I reached for a collection of bottles lined up on a shelf above me. Faint floral and citrusy aromas from shampoos and conditioners tickled my nose when I opened them. I grabbed an ivory comb and started carefully working through the knots in my hair, feeling its texture change from coarse hay to silky velvet as I untangled it. With each pass of the comb, I felt less like a discarded animal and more like a person again.

My skin was flushed pink when I finally climbed out of the water. It was the best bath of my life, and I couldn't help but wonder, had he drawn it for me? Or did he have a servant do it?

The Demon's failure to provide me with clean clothing after bathing caused my sense of cleanliness to deteriorate.

Whatever. I was too tired to care.

My body felt heavy and drained as I sank into the plush mattress and let out a sigh. My eyelids drooped and I fell into a deep sleep almost instantly.

Startled awake by the sound of a lock turning, followed by the door cracking open, I sat up in bed, rubbing the sleep out of my eyes. However long my nap was, it left me more tired than not.

The Demon strode into the room, grasping what seemed to be garments and a fresh pair of boots. He placed them all on an ornate wooden chair beside the bed before turning his gaze on me. His eyes resembled black holes, his facial expression inscrutable.

Panic rose in my chest, and I crawled away from him until I was pressed against the headboard. "What do you want?" I attempted to sound tough, but my fear made my voice quaver.

"Like I told you, you don't have control of this situation." His knee hit the mattress, and I almost screamed.

"Tell me, dickhead," I spat out. "What are you going to do with me?"

Raising his arms above his head, he grasped the top of the bed's canopy. His muscles flexed beneath his shirt, drawing attention to how attractive he was—but that was beside the point. "You ask a lot of questions for someone who is being held captive."

"I refuse to just lie here and let your wicked minions manipulate and hurt me." The words were barely audible, betraying my unease. Tired, hungry, homesick—horrified by the situation I found myself in—no matter how hard I tried to stay brave, fear always found a way in.

As I watched him meticulously peruse me, his eyes filled with a labyrinth of impenetrable intentions, my fear turned into overwhelming horror.

He wanted something, and I had a good idea of what that something was.

"Wouldn't you rather not know what I'm doing with you?" He sneered. "You may survive better if you don't. No jitters of anticipation. Sometimes, it's better to just stay in the dark."

What a piece of evil shit. Rage burned in my blood, snuffing out the fear. I wanted to tell him off. I wanted to fight him or, better yet, kill him. Tipping my chin up, I looked at him with as much disdain as I could muster. "Maybe for you. I come from a place where there's no darkness, you jerk."

He chuckled, his eyes twinkling with amusement. "Well," he said, bringing down his arms. I watched as he unbuttoned his jacket. "I've always found it strange that your realm has no night. How would you ever appreciate the light if you've never tasted darkness?"

The people I grew up with seemed happy, but I couldn't help but feel like their smiles were forced. Including mine. Like we just went about our lives pretending to be content with the cards we'd been dealt. Yes, life was good for us, however, there was plenty of darkness that lurked in the shadows beyond the castle walls. We may have been shielded from it by living in the royal court, but that didn't stop me from wondering what else was out there.

We stared at each other, his penetrating gaze unnerving me. He knew his words had pierced me.

I couldn't bear to look up, so I focused on the texture of the mattress beneath me.

"Take off your clothes."

My head snapped back up so fast it made my neck hurt. "What?"

"You heard me."

A thunderous roar echoed through the room as I unleashed my anger. My voice reverberated off the walls. "Who do you think you are expecting me to undress in front of you? Think again, Demon. If you make one move towards me, I will ensure your life is not worth living." There was no hesitation in my threat. Our eyes locked in a battle of wills, and I refused to look away.

His face burned with defiance as he placed his meticulously folded jacket on the back of an elaborate chair and prowled toward me. My muscles tightened with renewed fear as I watched him pull his dagger and approach the head of the bed until he stood inches away.

"What are you doing?" My voice was firm but with an edge of fright as I scooted on my knees to the other edge of the mattress, desperate to get away from him. I put one foot on the ground, but he was fast, snatching up my dress and hauling me back onto the bed. He trapped my legs between his thighs as he sat back, dagger in hand, eyes intense and calculating.

A whimper tore out of me as I tried to sit up and escape, but he wouldn't budge, hovering over me until our faces were but inches away. "Stay still."

"Fuck you!"

The smirk on his full lips made my blood boil. "I just may take you up on that."

My body froze, though I couldn't deny my insides burned with the intrusive images playing in my mind. "You wish."

He chuckled but said nothing as he once again sat up above me, dagger in hand. "Stubborn little creature." That's all he said before he swept the blade down the center of my bustier, from top to bottom, until the fabric fell away at my sides, revealing my breasts to him.

"What in tarnation!" I bucked with all my strength, trying to get him off me, but it was no use. "I'll scream!"

"No one will hear you, nor will they care."

I writhed, trying to sit up, but he scooted further up my body until his knees clamped on either side of my rib cage. The dread in my veins was unimaginable, but my disappointment was just as palpable, because a part of me thought he was better than this. That he wouldn't be capable of violating someone, even if he was bad enough to kidnap and cause bodily harm.

Rip.

With the bustier gone, he scooted back down to my legs, cutting off my belt, skirt, and undergarments as he went.

Tears slid down my face as I braced for the inevitable. He'd win, but I would go down fighting, and maybe twist his balls so hard I'd leave him barren for the rest of his miserable life. "Get. The. Fuck. Off. Me."

He said nothing, instead sheathing the dagger before taking each half of my dress and finishing to rip it off me, until I was naked.

His hungry gaze roved over me, lingering on my breasts. The hard bob of his Adam's apple revealed his arousal.

And even though I didn't want what he was about to do, I was wet between the legs. Although it seemed crazy, I had a desire for him, but I also wanted to have a choice in the matter. I'd never be fine with being forced, and I knew if he ever tried to violate me, my attraction toward him would disappear.

The Demon hovered over me, planting his hands on either side of my head. I readied myself to fight back. My heart raced in my chest as his face got closer, the air around us tightening with tension. He looked at me, his vibrant green eyes glinting dangerously as shadows crept across his features. His low growl was so powerful, it felt like a physical force pushing against me, and I knew I'd never experienced such raw masculinity before.

His raw sensuality was overwhelming, and I had to bite my lip to keep from moaning out loud.

"Now be a good little girl for me and get dressed."

REAVER

I STARED UNAPOLOGETICALLY.

I'd seen many naked females in my one hundred and thirty-one years of life—both women I bedded and the Mystics I captured to fulfill my father and uncle's plans to take over the realms.

But as I watched her get off the bed, face flushed and eyes enraged, I couldn't deny this female had a body that defied space and time. Her skin, smooth and tan from the sun, her hair bright like Aurora, falling in luscious locks around her shoulders, and those damn tits my mouth was watering over.

She fixed me with a stare that could cut glass, her fury palpable. One hand trying to cover her breasts, the other covering that sweet spot between her legs.

I didn't know her name, but it didn't matter. With those looks, her foul mouth, and that delicious scent, she was the most enticing female I'd ever met, and my cock was begging me to do something about it.

"Turn around."

Her request was so asinine, I quirked an eyebrow. I'd cut her clothes off her body and my eyes had feasted on her beauty, so why would she want to hide from me now?

Crossing my arms, I let my gaze rake over her delicious body.

The growl that came out of her was so fierce, my erection swelled in my trousers, her feistiness was an aphrodisiac. "Turn the hell around or I won't get dressed."

I wasn't opposed to her staying naked, but Murmur was waiting.

My steps echoed in the room as I stalked closer and closer to her. My prey. She shrank back against the wall. Smirking, I placed my hands on either side of her head and leaned in close, savoring the way she trembled beneath me. Those beautiful blue eyes were mesmerizing—even more so now that fear and rage filled them. "I think you haven't grasped the full meaning of captivity yet," I whispered menacingly. "There's no escape from this fate. You belong to us now, doomed to serve my father and uncle until your dying day."

Her breath became ragged, eyes widening. I wanted to feel elated by it, but a sliver of guilt squirmed beneath my skin, leaving me unable to celebrate the moment. My heart constricted, as if wrung dry by the sheer power of her dread. The unfamiliar emotion sent a shiver of discomfort through my body.

"What do you mean? What kind of service?"

"I think you know."

I'd been taught to believe I was a bad person, and no amount of beauty or kindness could ever make me capable of anything beyond sex, death, and destruction. But when I gazed upon this lovely yet exasperating creature, something unexpected stirred inside me, and I found myself being pulled toward her as if by an invisible tether.

Her presence ignited a craving within me. On one hand, I wanted to act as I had with everyone else in my life—cold and without feeling. But I also yearned for something different.

I yearned to protect her.

It scared me more than my uncle or father did. I felt the urge to retaliate and discipline her for evoking these emotions in me.

Letting go of her need for modesty, she pushed me away, her warm hands on my chest making me want to bend her over and do unspeakable things to her. "I'm not a whore and I'll never be one." She pushed me harder, effectively backing me up. "You didn't even mean to kidnap me!" Push. "I'm just the stupid girl you had to bring along."

I let her continue to push me backward, unwilling to tell her the truth; that her abduction wasn't accidental, though I wasn't privy to my uncle's reason for wanting the mortal maid.

Yet, she is not a mortal being.

"I'd rather die than do what you're insinuating."

Snatching her wrists off my chest, I pulled her forward until her tits pushed up against my shirt. She tried to pull away, so I wrapped an arm around her waist. Damn, her skin was soft. My cock was raging in my trousers, and a crazy desire to kiss her enveloped me, which I found strange because I didn't kiss. I mostly had sex with mortal prostitutes, as it was the best way to fulfill my physical needs without involving feelings. So, not only did I not kiss, but the women I frequented had a no-kissing rule. It was a win-win. But as I took in this insanely sexy and fierce female, I couldn't help but want to devour her.

I splayed a hand over her lower back. "Yes, it's true you just piggybacked onto your princess's kidnapping. But you may have just as much value."

"How? How am I valuable to your uncle, whoever that is?"

"You don't know who my uncle is?"

"Of course not," she hissed. "I didn't even know I was in Raetia!" She looks up at me through thick eyelashes, a sheepish look on her face. "Am I even in Raetia?"

I concealed a smirk, frustrated by how endearing I found her insecurities. "Yes."

"So, who the fuck is your uncle?"

Her dirty mouth was so enticing. "Murmur is my uncle; Malthus is my father."

Her face paled, and she looked like she might faint. "The Demon King." Her voice was but a whisper, her breathing heavy and erratic.

"One of them. My father is also a king."

"That makes you… a prince of The Abyss."

"I prefer Prince of Hell."

She looked up at me with large eyes. Her voice quivered as she spoke. "What does he want with me? I'm a nobody."

I smiled, bending down to meet her gaze. I ran a finger down the length of her jaw. "Ah, but you are a somebody, aren't you, Little Creature?"

She shook her head and blurted out in protest. "I have no powers. I'm just a stupid mortal female with nothing to offer except for gardening skills and healing elixirs!"

She was so frantic I let her go, watching as she paced the room, arms flailing about her, as if she'd forgotten she was naked. Not that I was complaining. I frowned. Did she not know? My eyes guzzled on her supple curves. "You are female, but mortal, you are not."

She huffed. "I beg to differ." Turning to face me, she waved a disapproving finger at me, as if I was a child she'd caught red-handed in the biscuit jar. "Don't lie to me. You don't even know what you're talking about. You don't know me."

I grabbed her finger, then her wrist, once again pulling her until our bodies were flushed. Lowering my head, I trailed my nose over the smooth skin of her elegant neck, delighting in the shiver she gave. "I may not know you, but I can smell you, and you don't smell like any mortal I've ever met."

Her eyes widened in shock. She thought she was some mortal with no Mystic ability.

Her scent threw me into a tailspin. It was unmatched by Mystics or mortals. It made me impossibly hard. Still gripping her tight, I ground my hardness against her quivering body. "Now get dressed, before I lose all control and fuck you against the wall."

When I lifted my head to look at her, I could swear her eyes had glazed over with lust. But then she gritted her teeth, her nostrils flaring and frown creased, an internal battle raging in her expression.

Bloody hell, I wanted her. But my uncle awaited, and there was a reason I was his number one, even above his own son.

I let her go and stepped back, jamming both hands into the pockets of my trousers. "You are no mortal, but you are also not nameless. I think it's time you tell me your name."

She scoffed, rolling her eyes. "Why would I do that?"

"Because you're my captive. Give me your name."

"Why should I give you mine when you haven't given me yours?"

Fuck, she was infuriating. I'd had no one stand up to me this way besides Ruslan.

She was so strong, nothing like the whimpering mess of a princess she served and protected.

Regardless of the secrets she kept about her identity, I had an intuition that her presence here was fated. There was something special about her.

"Reaver."

Her eyebrows shot up. "What?"

"My name is Reaver."

A flush crawled up her chest and face, like my name turned her on, which made me even harder.

I didn't care enough to hide my reaction from her. She stared at the tent in my trousers. Her cheeks reddened, and she frowned. "You're disgusting."

I corked an eyebrow. "You don't look disgusted," I said, my gaze taking in her stiff nipples.

She huffed in frustration, covering them with her hands, as if she hadn't spent the last five minutes unabashedly naked in front of me. "Just turn around."

Not happening.

"No. Get used to it, princess."

Her breathing escalated, jagged and uncomfortable, yet strangely captivating, as her chest moved rhythmically, her olive skin causing my mouth to water.

The enjoyment I felt from causing her anxiety made me aware of my cruelty. Despite my longing to protect her, I'd never be what she deserved.

Suddenly, she closed her eyes, took a deep breath, and when she reopened them, the fierceness was back.

I remained silent, watching as she bent over, giving me a glorious view of her ass, as she picked up the garments laid out for her to wear. She brought the black leather corset up into the light, turning it this way and that as if she didn't know what it was.

Spinning to face me, she waved the corset in my face. "What is this, and how am I supposed to put this on?"

"It's a corset." I sighed. "Come here."

She remained rooted in place.

I stalked toward her and snatched the corset out of her hand. "You are the most maddening female I've ever met."

Squaring her shoulders and tilting her chin up, she stared at me. "And you are the most annoying male I've ever met."

I chuckled. "Lift your arms."

"Why?"

"Because I'm going to dress you."

REETAH

UN MELT ME.

My gulp was audible, and I knew he'd heard it by the amused glint in his eyes.

"Because I'm going to dress you."

The nerve endings throughout my body were on fire and I was falling down a lustful rabbit hole which threatened to rob me of common sense and every shred of self-preservation I possessed.

Reaver—Goddess, why did his name have to be so sexy—was a bad guy. And not just any bad guy, but a fucking prince of hell. And yet… I let him get close and take the weird garment from my hand.

Mesmerized, I watched as he set it down on the back of the chair, instead picking up a long strip of fabric, which he then wrapped around me. I obeyed his every command as he dressed me in the most exquisite clothing, the style so different from mine, but no less flattering.

Goosebumps exploded on my skin as the pads of his strong fingers glided over it, ever so lightly. Goddess, he was a bad guy, but he didn't take advantage of me, and he was gorgeous, dominant, and confident. His scent made me want to do very naughty things to him.

"You don't smell like any mortal I've ever met."

I considered myself mortal since I'd displayed no Mystic powers. If the empowerment—the process through which Mystics came into their power—hadn't yet hit me at twenty-five, I doubted it would ever come. I had resigned myself to the reality that the mystical genes of my ancestors had skipped my generation, as it had skipped so many before me.

My heart pounded fast in my chest as I stood in front of him, letting him dress me. He wrapped the leather corset around my torso, coming to stand close behind me. "Walk to the bed."

"What? Why?"

Patience was not a virtue for him because he moved me until I stood in front of the bed. "Hold on to the bedpost."

Not waiting for me to comply, Reaver pulled at the silk laces threading through the back of the corset. All I could do was hold on to the bedpost and beg my body to behave as he expertly tightened the garment. He did it a little too well because I thought I'd pass out. "I can't breathe," I heaved.

The laces loosened, allowing my lungs to re-inflate. Once he was done, he turned me to face him. "Come here." Unwilling to wait for an answer, he took my hand and pulled me forward, his big, warm hand enveloping mine.

Fuck me, he was hot, and not just physically. His dominance was the stuff of wet dreams. Once we got to the chair, he picked up a black, lacy garter and a pair of matching panties. My breath hitched at the sight of this ridiculously handsome male holding the sexy fabric he planned to put on me.

I should've protested, should've pushed him away. But his eyes held me captive, promising me so many things, and there was nothing I could do but stare back.

With one knee on the ground, Reaver took my foot, placing it on his other knee as he then slid the panties up one leg and then the other.

The sexual tension thickening the air in the room suffocated me. I put my hands on his shoulders to keep my balance, my clit throbbing as he pulled the panties over my hips. His eyes darkened as he stared at my pussy with no shame, then licked his lips, making a strangled sound in his throat, like he was suppressing a groan.

Fuck, I was on fire and so entranced when he stood, I almost lost my balance, but he caught me by the waist and I felt like I could climax right then, the feel of his proximity and big warm hand on me almost too much to handle. Reaver leaned into me, his intoxicating scent filling my nostrils, as he reached behind me to grab a garter belt, before proceeding to clasp it around my waist with both hands. The shiver that went through me proved impossible to hide, and his lustful stare was the only acknowledgment he gave me. I was too turned on to be embarrassed by my reaction to him.

Dropping back down on one knee, Reaver took my foot, sliding it into a sheer stocking with a lacy band at the top. It was beautiful, and despite my circumstances, I felt sexy in a way I never had before. My sense of confidence took on an unfamiliar edge, and I wanted to deny myself that I wanted this man and all the danger he brought with him. It was exhilarating.

His stare never wavered as he rolled the other stocking on. I stared right back, my body sizzling under his scrutiny.

Sliding his hands over my upper thighs, he clipped the lacy tops to the garter. The urge to open my legs wider and guide his hand up my center was difficult to control, as was the shaking of my thighs under his maddening and confident touch.

Blazes, I was in trouble, not only because of the situation I found myself in, but because I was figuring out I liked a bad guy. I liked the bad guy.

What did that make me?

He stood, picking up another garment from the chair behind me. A long shiny skirt he wrapped around my waist under the corset. Then, his hand climbed up my thigh, bringing the front of the skirt with it, like he was about to touch me there. I wanted him to. Goddess, how I wanted him to touch me everywhere.

But common sense seeped back into my consciousness, and I knew I had to resist. "What are you doing?" My voice was low and gritty and nothing like how I wanted it to sound.

He didn't reply, simply gazing into my eyes and smirking before looking down, rolling the front of my skirt and tying each side to the leather straps dangling from the bottom of the corset. That's when I remembered the women I'd seen outside when I'd tried to run away. Some of them wore their skirt the same way. Stepping back, he crossed his thick arms over his chest and scanned me from top to bottom; the approval on his face undeniable. I melted, and common sense left me once more. If he'd tackled me and taken me to bed, my objection would have been non-existent.

Instead, he went to the door and opened it, speaking to who I assumed was the guard, and then closed it, looking back at me. "Someone will come in to do your hair and makeup." And with that, he grabbed his jacket off the back of the chair and turned to leave.

"Great, I guess it wouldn't hurt to look my best while a bunch of asshole Demons take turns having their way with me," I said, my voice dripping with contempt.

His eyes shone with deviant amusement. "I will return for you and take you to the king."

Dammit. I wished he was the one inflicting pain or whatever else they had planned. Hunching my shoulders, I folded my arms crossed over my chest, now emphasized by the deep plunge of the corset's neckline, a garment seemingly capable of performing some kind of magic trick to make my breasts look bigger. His gaze flickered downward, lingering slightly too long.

"I'm not interested in meeting Murmur, the king of assholes."

"Let me make something clear. Your interests are of little concern to me."

I glared. "What about Emmaline?"

"The princess isn't your problem anymore."

"The hell she isn't." I dropped my arms, fisting my hands with all my indignation. "She will always be my problem."

He frowned, staring at me as if pondering something. "Why are you so loyal to her? Aren't you tired of being a maid and a servant to this capricious, spoiled child?"

Scoffing, I opened my mouth to speak, closed it, opened it again, and then shut it completely because his words had left me reeling. Which only made him keep going.

"I would think you'd be happy to be rid of her by now."

"I'll never be happy to be rid of her. I don't consider myself a maid or a servant. She's my best friend. She's the sister I never had, and you're going to let her go."

He threw his head back with laughter, and it sounded so fucking good I wanted to be buried with the sound in a perpetual loop. Something was definitely wrong with me.

"You sure have big balls for such a defenseless little mortal as you pretend to be. But don't worry. I will torture the powers out of you. I'll make you hurt so badly you'll have no choice but to use your abilities in self-defense, finally revealing yourself to me. And then, I'll make you yearn for my cock until you want nothing else out of your miserable life but to be fucked by me." He drew my face nearer to his, our noses touching. "And fuck you, I will."

I never knew fear and arousal could coexist. The evidence was in the wetness between my legs. I didn't bother telling I truly had no powers. "In your dreams."

"Then let's end this charade and get moving. Once the king meets you, we'll figure out how to use you."

I sucked in a harsh breath. "As if you don't already know, I'm about to become a bloody sex slave."

A flash of discomfort crossed his face before his shadows retreated and he let go of my face. My legs wobbled when my high-heeled feet hit the ground and I almost lost my balance but he steadied me with a firm hand to my shoulder, which only annoyed me more. "If you have powers, whatever they may be, I'm sure they can be put to good use." He waited, as if he knew I wanted to ask more, so out of sheer stubbornness, I remained silent despite the questions clawing at me to come out.

He grinned, seeing right through me. "Murmur is amassing an army of Mystics."

"Why?"

"He wants to conquer all the realms, including the Island of Anathema."

I chuckled because what he was saying was preposterous. "No one can do that. Aurora would never allow it."

"No one has seen the Goddess in a millennium because Aurora doesn't exist. It's a myth. A joke."

"Well, that may be true, but the Angels would never allow it."

"More and more Angels are turning dark. Falling from the Auroran City. And if they go dark long enough, they turn into Demons."

My jaw dropped. I'd heard of this before, but the people in my realm loved to kiss Angel ass, so no one believed it. "That's not true."

"Oh? Well, I guess you're right. After all, who am I to speak on the matter? I'm only the spawn of a fallen Angel."

"What?"

"Yes. My father is one. Murmur was a fallen Angel, too. And look at him now."

The blood drained from my face. Everyone in my realm always put so much faith in the Angels, believing they were our only hope against the Stygian's darkness. "No way," I whispered.

"Yes way. Don't count on the Angels. They won't be there for you. This is an easy fight. Murmur has had no rivals. No one is standing up to him."

"I'm not bowing to him."

"Do you really believe a puny mortal is going to stand up to the mighty King of the Abyss?"

"The mighty King of The Abyss?" I quirked an eyebrow, unable to believe my ears. "Isn't that Luc?"

"You don't believe fallen Angels exist, but you believe in Luc?"

I said nothing because he was challenging everything my parents and the royals had taught me. "I was told Luc was not a fallen Angel, but the first Demon, made by Aurora to create balance in the world."

He sighed and looked at me as if I was the most ignorant person in existence. "Luc was the first monarch of The Abyss, due to him being the first Archangel to drop from Heaven. But many more followed in his footsteps, each with their own legions made up of demons, ready to obey all their orders. Murmur will be the ruler of every realm, wielding the strength of the Stygian within him."

Pressing my lips together, I tried to contain my laughter, failing miserably as it roared up my throat, tumbling out of my mouth unceremoniously. The ridiculousness of what he was saying fueled my giggles. But he didn't crack a smile or show even a hint of amusement.

I sobered. "You're being serious?"

"Of course I'm being serious."

"No one can absorb the power of the Stygian. This is absolutely preposterous, not to mention suicidal."

His chuckle was deep, running over my skin like soft wool. I thanked the Goddess he couldn't see the quake his voice caused inside me. "I guess you'll have to stick around and see."

"Stick around? Are you nuts?"

He frowned, staring at me as if I had snakes dancing in my hair.

I continued, "The only way I'll stick around is if you keep me here, which you won't be able to do for much longer, because I promise you, I will escape, and when I do, you—"

All my laughter fled in a rush the moment Reaver grabbed the back of my neck and crashed his mouth to mine. His lips were pillowy-soft and full, and I wanted so much to melt and give in because it was already the best kiss of my life, which was pathetic, but I'd never been kissed with so much passion.

Logical thought kicked in when I felt his wet hot tongue glide over my lips, trying to get me to open for him.

Fuck that. Planting both hands on his chest, I pushed him away, though I felt the chill brought on by our disconnection.

"What the fuck is wrong with you?"

"I had to shut you up somehow."

"Listen, asshole, I will never want you, so don't ever do—"

He came at me again, dropping his jacket to the floor before moving his hand to my throat, the other fisting my hair. I tried to keep my lips shut tight, but it was no use. This man undid me like no other. I moaned, melting into his body, my hands clinging to his black shirt. And my mouth? It let him in like he was the oxygen I needed to breathe. As if I'd die if I didn't bend to his desires.

The gentle pressure of his lips transformed into one of urgency, sending a jolt of desire through my veins. His strong hand moved from my hair to my ass, tugging me closer as he growled in pleasure, grinding into me. The electric pulse between us was so intense I thought I would melt right there in his arms.

I was ready for him to do everything and more. But he broke the kiss, leaving me swaying and struggling to regain my composure. "You want me."

"Fuck off."

He grinned, squeezing my throat a little more. "You better behave or you'll face the consequences."

He bent down to pick up his jacket, swinging it over his shoulder as he strode toward the door.

"Consequences, shmonsequences," I muttered, but unfortunately not quiet enough because he spun around to face me. He fixed me with a steady, appraising gaze as he shook his head, a glimmer of amusement lingering in his eyes before a dazzling smile broke his stern demeanor. The sight was almost too much for me to take and I felt my chest tighten with an unfamiliar longing. I wanted to pry every laugh and every smile out of him.

The female who came to groom me was older, serious, and most likely mute, as she didn't speak a word the whole time she did my hair, nails, and makeup. No one had ever pampered me this much, and yet, I couldn't enjoy it, as what had happened with Reaver kept playing on a loop in my head. The fear, the shock of him cleaning me and dressing me. The arousal this had caused. And that kiss.

Best kiss of my life. It's a shame that his final words rekindled my hatred for him.

"You better behave or else you'll face the consequences."

Fuck him. I would do the opposite of behave.

REETAH

A SHIVER RAN DOWN MY SPINE AS I FOLLOWED him down the long corridor. Large stained-glass windows on either side caused a prism of colors to fall on my skin. It should have warmed me. It should have made me feel better. But it didn't.

My skin broke out into goosebumps as I fidgeted with the ruffles of my skirt—which I could no longer enjoy or feel sexy wearing, seeing as how I was about to meet the big bad wolf.

I was angry that Reaver made me wear something that made me feel good, despite knowing what awaited me.

Petrified, I slowed my steps as we approached a large black door that seemed made of marble.

What was on the other side? I couldn't picture it. All I knew was that Murmur was waiting, and I could sense the impending danger that lingered in the air. He'd most likely violate me or order his minions to do it for him.

I wasn't sure they'd kill me, although I wouldn't put it past them. But there are worse things than death. I thought about Emmie, wondered if they'd already done these things to her. My thoughts flitted to what he'd said about her, words which had unwittingly resonated with me.

My bond with my best friend was complicated. I loved her, but I often felt like she took more from me than she gave. I was always the one to take action while she would be the person in need of rescuing. What would it be like if our roles were reversed? If we connected through our mutual strengths rather than me repeatedly being her savior?

Regardless of the nuances of our bond, the Demon was wrong in one regard: I'd always be loyal to Emmie, and I wouldn't stop until we were both back in our realm.

But where was she?

The thought of returning to that dreadful dungeon made my breath tremble, a wave of dizziness causing me to halt my steps. I observed his powerful strides and solid build, oblivious to my stillness. Maybe he wouldn't even notice. Maybe he'd just walk in there without me and I could make a run for it. I rolled my eyes. Sure enough, ten paces ahead, he stopped, barely turning his head over his shoulder as he leered at me.

"Move."

I sucked in a breath, startled by the command in his voice, which attracted me and terrified me all at once. I remained rooted to the spot, my heard speeding as I watched him make his way back to me.

He stared me down, eyes cold as ice. "Whatever happens in there, keep your mouth shut. Understood?"

I pursed my lips, attempting to suppress my rebellious side, but it refused to be silenced. "It's not like I have anything to say. I don't have any secrets to divulge to them."

He rolled his eyes, sighing like I was an insolent child. "That's not what I mean."

"Then what do you mean?"

He got in my face. "Don't talk back or you may find yourself in a worse situation than the one already awaiting you."

Staring into the depth of his eyes, I saw the seriousness of his warning. His gaze softened, and he brought a hand to my face, running his fingers through a strand of my hair and gently tucking it behind my ear. The gesture was so caring that I wondered if at least some part of him wanted to help me. Was he concerned for me?

I gave him a subtle nod, throat dry and fingers clammy. He let me go, his vicious façade dropping back in place as we turned the corner, stopping in front of a set of large black doors.

Ominous.

My vision blurred even before we entered the room.

Keep it together, Ree.

Reaver gestured to the two guards who stood on either side of the door and I watched as they opened it.

I took a deep inhale, willing my eyes to dry. As we walked into the room, I vowed to never show weakness in front of Murmur and his legion.

A male sat behind a luxurious desk, tall—enormous, actually—with long silver hair tucked behind pointy ears. I pondered whether Reaver had pointy ears too, and suddenly, my hand yearned to reach out and expose his hair to satisfy my curiosity.

Pushing the shadow Demon out of my head and refocused on Murmur. His skin was so pallid it seemed to glow in the dim light, and he wore an all-black suit with blood-red trim. His finger bore a large golden signet ring that glinted ominously in the candlelight. I could sense the power radiating from him—he was no ordinary Demon, but a king of hell.

An ancient being created by Aurora before the Stygian had obliterated his light, turning him into darkness itself. Purity turned into pure evil.

And he exuded just that. Pure evil.

Murmur remained focused on the stack of papers before him, not bothering to lift his gaze. "What do you want, Reaver?"

Reaver stood stiffly next to me, a hand on the small of my back, which I disturbingly found comfort in.

"The extra girl," he declared before walking over to the side of the desk and standing still in front of the window overlooking the street. He kept his hands clasped behind his back, standing rigidly as if awaiting orders from his uncle, like all the other people in the room. Watching him surrender control was unsettling.

The extra girl. I couldn't believe it. My insides were boiling with a mix of emotions—anger, confusion, and an overwhelming sense of betrayal, even though Reaver owed me no loyalty. I wanted to scream at the top of my lungs, but I stayed silent and kept my head down.

Murmur's head snapped up, and he looked at Reaver for a second before his gaze landed on me with no expression, his eyes black as onyx. He eyed me up and down, taking in the outfit Reaver had put me in.

With my back straight, my shoulders squared, and my chin up, I stared right back, drawing confidence from the outfit, because I refused to let him intimidate me.

"Hmm," he said, steepling his fingers under his chin like a pompous douche. "She's an unexpected surprise and a pretty one as well, but I have little use for her. After all, she is mortal. Is she not?"

Reaver's jaw tensed as Murmur uttered his suspicions that I was no mortal. His response was stiff. "Yes, you still wanted to meet her though so here she is, as requested."

An undertone of annoyance was evident in his words, but Murmur appeared to be oblivious or simply disregarded it.

Murmur stood, his fancy wooden chair scraping behind him. He rounded his desk and came to stand directly in front of me. He had to be at least seven feet tall. I'd seen nothing like it before.

"What's your name, girl?"

I remained quiet, rebelliously withholding my name.

A loud crack echoed through the entire room as his massive hand flew through the air like a blur before crashing into my face. The force of the impact sent me reeling backwards, my vision clouding as intense heat spread across my skin. Pain echoed through my head and pulsed in my ears. The metallic taste of blood invaded my mouth.

I wanted to cry out, but bit down on my lower lip, forcing myself to remain composed. Lifting a trembling hand, I gently prodded at my already swollen cheek.

Glancing up, I met Reaver's gaze, desperately searching for solace in his eyes.

His vision grew more focused and his mouth contorted into a scowl. With hands curled into tight fists, his expression turned menacing, as if he wanted to draw the pistol from his belt and shoot Murmur with it. But then he calmed himself, the angry expression replaced by one of nonchalance.

Murmur smirked. "I admire your bravery, though it is ultimately foolish, as I have no qualms about hurting a weak mortal."

With my hand on my throbbing cheek, I glared, despite the quaking of my legs.

"Tell the King your name," Reaver demanded, all traces of the intimacy we'd shared gone from his voice. He sounded as cold as his evil uncle.

The king. A self-proclaimed king held no credence. And he wasn't mine.

Focus on self-preservation.

"Reetah."

Murmur smirked. "Well, Reetah, it seems you're smarter than I thought you'd be."

I remained silent, chomping on my inner cheek to avoid making a stupid and fatal mistake.

"I hear you're the lady's maid to your princess, correct?"

"Yes."

"And yet you seem to have more of a backbone than the princess you've vowed to serve with your breath. So much loyalty for such a dreadfully dull and cowardly princess. Why is that?"

I kept my mouth shut.

"Very well, I'll allow you that secret." He walked back around his desk and sat, once again steepling his stupid fingers under his chin. "Are you sure you're mortal?"

"Yes. I'm just an earth witch."

He quirked an eyebrow, his interest piqued. "So you're not mortal."

"I'm not a magical witch. Earth witch is just a fancy term for healer. I just make elixirs that help people heal."

His stare on me was impassive. "How dull."

He rapped his long, pale fingers on the mahogany desk. "Well, you are beautiful. But alas, you're mortal, and elixirs won't be enough to heal my people when the war comes and we conquer the Angels, find Aurora and shred her to pieces the way she deserves."

I swallowed. Goddess, he was maniacal.

"But there is something I can use you for. After all, I'm not just gathering an army. I have current endeavors that require me to keep some people… happy."

I knew where he was going with this, and the horror of this knowledge made every fiber in my body tremble.

He watched me with keen black eyes, and a devious grin spread on his face. "Yes. You do know where you are, don't you, girl?"

"I'm in your house."

"Indeed, but this place is much more than that. The Villa, as we like to refer to it, is a pleasure house of sorts." He flicked his head toward where Reaver stood. "My nephew here is in charge of finding girls, usually magical, and bringing them here for... servitude."

The shadow Demon remained indifferent to my intense glare.

Murmur chuckled darkly. "See, in this manner, we've managed to accrue an army of the most powerful Mystics in the realms, some of them tasked with providing sexual services to Mystic and mortals alike. For some reason that I'll never understand, Angels gave the reins of the realms to feeble mortals, when they not only didn't deserve it, but were utterly unequipped for the job."

My heart raced so fast and yet its loud pounding in my ears wasn't enough to drown out his words and the weight of my new reality. I wanted to vomit.

"Those pompous mortals are so full of themselves, they cannot see that while we wine and dine them and throw the most beautiful men and women to fuck them and fulfill their every pathetic desire, I'm gathering information and finding out their weaknesses."

I'd fallen into the underbelly of a sick and twisted world I never knew existed, and it was far darker than I could've ever imagined.

"I'm preparing to take them all down, and now you'll help me achieve my goal."

"Please don't do this. You said you only recruit Mystics." I never begged, but I'd do it now with no shame because what he wanted to do with me was way worse than death.

My pleading words only made him sneer. "You'd be a great plaything for one of them, or more, depending on how many pay me for your services."

My heart raced as I felt the walls close in around me. My breath hitched in my throat and I wanted to scream, but no sound would come out. "And if I refuse?"

His cruel laughter filled the air, reverberating through the vast space until all that was left was an empty echoing void. "What makes you think you have free will? The moment Reaver took you, you ceased to be anything but my captive. So, if I tell you to bend over that is exactly what you will do. You can't refuse, and even if you could, I would not recommend it, as the first person who will pay for your resistance will be your cowardly princess."

He waved a hand dismissively. "You may leave, Reaver, and take her back to her cell. Perhaps she needs to be groomed some more. Get someone to teach her manners. And then you can throw her to the wolves."

BEETAH

The minute I stepped out of Murmur's office, my legs felt like jelly and the fear which had been slowly building in my chest was suffocating me. The heavy wooden doors closed behind me, trapping me in a sea of darkness and despair.

My entire being recoiled the moment I felt his hand on my lower back.

"Don't. Touch. Me!" My words sounded strained, my legs moving faster, desperately trying to put as much distance between myself and Murmur's shadow Demon. The memories of earlier, when I'd let him dress me and touch me and kiss me made me want to vomit with self-disgust.

Surprisingly, he heeded my demand, the warmth of his masculine hand leaving my skin cold and exposed to the darkness of this awful house.

The Villa.

A seedy establishment where those of questionable morality went to act out their most nefarious desires, unaware that they were being spied on.

What a bunch of idiots.

"Reetah." His voice sounded strangled, as if he was overcome with emotion that sounded much like remorse. Or perhaps he was simply salivating with the need to tame me.

It was the first time my name had left his lips, and yet, it sounded like venom.

I refused to answer, instead picking up my pace, the sun shining through the stained-glass windows no longer warming me but making me want to scream with the frustration of what my life had become. With the need for the life-giving sun that had always calmed me, and was now too far out of reach. I wanted to break through the window just to reach it.

"Reetah, stop."

Ignoring him, I hurried away, the discomfort of the boots on my feet and the tightness of the corset making each step and breath a struggle.

The corridor felt never-ending, with the haunting presence of dark stone sculptures portraying Angels, mortals, and Demons on either side of every door. I knew that through those doors lay a world of sin and debauchery where unspeakable acts happened night after night.

The sculptures' eyes bore into me like cold, dead orbs. They were a lifeless picture symbolizing the inevitable, a glimpse into my future that left no doubt in my mind. If I had to spend the rest of my life in sexual servitude, it wouldn't just kill me—it would destroy every part of who I was until there was nothing left but a shell of pain and despair. It would be a desolate death, one that would kill my spirit long before it took my body.

I shuddered at the thought, feeling a newfound determination ignite within me. I'd never let myself become a broken, empty thing. I would fight with everything I had to break free from my oppressors and reclaim my life—no matter the cost.

From a short distance, the unmistakable creak of a door echoed, followed by the appearance of a male dressed in a black suit similar to Reaver's. His beauty was impossible to ignore. Short dark hair, vivid blue eyes, which were staring at me, forcing me to stop in my tracks. He scanned me from head to toe before glancing behind me, a guarded look on his face.

He greeted the Demon with a curt nod, "Reaver." I had no idea if he was also a Demon or a human being spied upon, but it didn't matter. If he was here, he wasn't up to anything good. His positive traits meant nothing in the face of the misdeeds that led him to this place.

"Vox," Reaver said from behind me, and the mere sound of his voice filled me with rage. When the male emerged from the bedroom, leaving the door slightly ajar, I was struck speechless by what I saw.

An Angel sat on the bed, her back to the door, her wings white and splendorous as a swan's. They were neatly folded, an everlasting quilt of soft feathers.

Her skin resembled porcelain, its delicate texture matching the vulnerability in her eyes as she glanced back at me over her bare shoulder. Her eyes were blue like a clear sky on a sunny day water. They brimmed with grief as she sat there with a look of abject hopelessness that ripped through me like a jagged knife.

Her face was breathtakingly beautiful, with high-set cheekbones and lips as soft and delicate as rose petals. Her hair shimmered like golden silk, and I blinked back tears at the sheer unfairness of it all.

She was blonde like me. My heart stopped, a sinking feeling settling in, as I realized what this meant—she was from Frentani!

My instincts took over and my feet moved faster than my brain could process, sprinting toward her as if in a trance. Reaver's firm hand clamped down on my arm, halting my progress. His body heat enveloped me and my rage burst forth like a volcano. With every ounce of energy I had left, I shoved him away and sprinted past the Angel's door, barely escaping his grasp.

"Bloom, shut the door," he bellowed, his authoritative tone filling the air.

Her name was Bloom. I imagined she once shone with unrivaled beauty—a radiant blossom of innocence and hope—until Murmur took her, casting her aside like a wilted flower, her petals crushed on the dungeon's dirt floor.

"Reetah!" Reaver's voice thundered like a raging storm, his ironclad arms coiling around my own like unbreakable chains, halting me in my tracks, his voice a combination of anger and an emotion I couldn't pinpoint.

I whirled around, my entire body shaking with fury, and I slammed my palms into his chest. "How could you?" My fists pounded on him, and I felt the tears rise as I unleashed all of my pent-up anger. The force of my rage mixed with deep sorrow caused me to scream out as hot tears poured down my face. "How could you?!"

He stood there like a mountain, his calm and towering presence defying the tempest of emotion I threw at him. His cold eyes were pinned on me, unyielding in the face of my rage. I unleashed every bit of hatred inside, my fists flying with reckless abandon as their fury collided with his body. Yet his expression stayed the same, a blank canvas devoid of any emotion.

"How could you be so heartless, so willing to serve such a monster!"

I watched as he flinched at my words, his gaze quickly shifting away from mine. It was the first time I'd seen something resembling shame written all over him.

"How many people have you taken? How many lives have you ruined?"

I knew my accusations made me seem self-righteous, but meeting Reaver's uncle had revealed the harsh reality of his profession. To hear that it was Reaver's job to abduct people and condemn them to such a cruel fate broke my heart because I'd thought there was good inside of him.

And the thought of him subjecting me to the same punishment was an agonizing torture. And Emmie... the mere thought of losing her tore at my heart with a vengeance. Oh Goddess, what would become of sweet, innocent Emmie?

"Look at me!" I shouted, raining down a flurry of punches on his body. He looked back and the expression I saw on his face was one of immense pain and suffering. For the briefest moment, a powerful, complex emotion illuminated his eyes, breaking through my anger—something powerful and pure. Something that made him more than the wicked Demon he portrayed so well. It reminded me of the way he'd acted when Murmur slapped me across the face.

But it was gone in a heartbeat, replaced by his carefully crafted mask of ice.

His fingers dug into my skin as if they were claws, piercing me with a fierce intensity. I could feel the heat radiating off of him as he thrust his face close to mine, gritting out through clenched teeth, "this is who I am and who I'll always be."

I shook my head defiantly. "I don't believe it. I refuse to believe it."

He bared his teeth in a sneer. "Why? Because you need to validate the fact that you crave me, even though I'm a monster?"

My chin trembled. "No, because I've seen the good in you."

"You've seen nothing but what I let you see," he snarled, "and your opinion means nothing to me."

He then hoisted me onto his shoulder like I was nothing. I didn't resist, too tired and defeated. I closed my eyes and let the tears fall. When we reached my new prison cell, he burst through the door, once again dropping me onto the bed.

With a last display of aggression, he slammed the door shut, leaving me in the eerie silence of darkness.

REAVER

"You know what to do?" Murmur said to the group of guards standing in front of him as I made my way into his office. I took a sip of whiskey from the tumbler in my hand, my other hand in the pocket of my slacks as the group of males all nodded their compliance.

"What to do with what?" I asked, making my way to his couch and sitting, setting an ankle over a knee.

"Train the mortal wench."

"With all due respect, Uncle, but are you sure? Wouldn't the princess be worth more with her virtue intact?"

"I'm referring to her nuisance of a lady's maid."

At this, my body stiffened, and I returned my foot to the floor, scooting closer to the edge of the couch. "What do you plan to do with her?"

"Have the boys here fuck her into oblivion, so she may learn how to please our clients." He turned to look at the men gathered in the room, their tongues almost wagging, no doubt imagining all the ways they would fuck her.

My fists tightened of their own accord, and I struggled to find the will not to rip said tongues out of their mouths and shove them down their throats.

"Is that really necessary?"

Uncle aimed his sharp eyes in my direction. "Is something the matter, nephew?"

"The girl is a weak mortal, hardly in need of extreme tactics to tame her into obedience." I tamped down a grimace as my words sounded false to my own ears. I didn't know what Reetah was, but mortal she was not. Of this, I was sure. I could feel it, and if I did, so did my uncle.

"You know better than anyone the girl is no mere mortal. What better way to trigger whatever abilities she may possess than by subjecting her to a bit of torture? It will scare her powers into manifesting themselves, and once we know what she's capable of, we can decide which role to give her in my brothel and in my army."

"Subjecting her to a bit of torture."

The statement sat on my chest with an all too foreign heaviness.

My jaw clenched as I did my best to maintain an air of impassivity, but my uncle had known me my whole life. There was no fooling him.

Murmur arched a powerful brow. "Is there something you're not telling me, Reaver?"

"I will take her for myself." The words flew out before I could grasp what they were, or the significance of my statement. I didn't ask him to give her to me. I simply informed him of my decision, disregarding his status as the King of Hell and future King of Anathema.

"You have been a faithful soldier, serving under my command for over a hundred years. For that, I will grant your request and pardon your insolence, but let me be clear when I say that not even my son has a right to speak to me as if it is he who holds the power. Let this be the first and only time you treat me as your subject, instead of the other way around."

"Yes, Your Highness." I stood and bowed to the bastard, before turning on my heel and walked to the door.

"Reaver."

"Yes?"

"Love isn't something I allow here. I don't know your reasons for wanting this girl for yourself, but it better not be love, and I expect to see evidence of her taming."

13

I FOUND MYSELF ALONE IN THE OPULENT BEDROOM, still elegantly dressed, and with no word as to what came for me next.

"And then, you can throw her to the wolves."

The words resonated in my brain, making me rattle with fear and uncertainty. I still hated Reaver but was grateful he brought me to this bedroom, despite Murmur ordering him to take me back to the dungeon.

I was to become a whore. Fancy and well-mannered, but a whore. Sex workers weren't uncommon in my realm, nor was it something looked down upon. But this wouldn't be sex work because there was no way in hell, I'd ever volunteer.

I brought my arms around my waist, seeking solace in the pressure against my body as I worked to steady my breaths. But it was hard. I'd longed for a different life for so long, but this was far from what I'd imagined.

The doorknob turned, and I stiffened, not knowing who would walk through the door. The moment I saw him, I expelled a relieved breath. I didn't know why. He was an asshole. He was a Demon. I should hate him. And I did. But somehow, once I confronted Murmur, Reaver seemed less dangerous. I knew I was fooling myself and this was a way for me to feel some modicum of comfort in such a bleak situation.

His stare was severe, face sharp and determined as he came to stand in front of me, fists at his sides. "Come with me."

"No."

His clenched jaw conveyed his frustration. Good.

"Murmur's underlings are on their way to the dungeon. When they see you're not there, they will come here. And once they have you, they will hurt you. You either come with me right now or wait for them, and trust me, they will not have any mercy on you." He turned on his heel and walked out.

Overcome with fear, I reluctantly followed, my body shaking in response. "Where are we going?"

"Stop asking questions and be grateful I came for you. No one else has the luck you've had since you arrived here."

"I didn't arrive here. You kidnapped me," I hissed.

He whirled on me with an icy glare, eyes smoldering with a lethal intensity. I froze in place as he advanced toward me, step by step, my heart pounding in my chest like a war drum. His massive body trapped me against the hallway wall, his hot breath fanning over my face. He leaned in, our faces mere inches apart, his deep and masculine scent surrounding me. "I won't offer you apologies for my actions," he hissed menacingly. "This is how I survive. This is who I am. Don't expect me to live in some fantasy land filled with sunshine and rainbows when all I've ever known is the darkness and depravity of this world."

I stared up at him, speechless.

"It's nothing personal. I kidnapped many before you." His nose ran over the shell of my ear, and he inhaled, eliciting a shiver from me. "And I'll definitely never regret taking you."

Oh, my Goddess.

After stepping away from me, he resumed walking, not waiting for me to join him. We walked to the opposite side of the manor, down long hallways and many closed doors. I saw no one except for guards. Why were there guards here but not in the dungeon? It made no sense.

And where was everyone else? I didn't see any prisoners or any of the mortal clients Murmur talked about. If this was a brothel, where were the moaning sounds and the pounding of bedframes against the walls?

We arrived in front of what looked like an intricate birdcage-like structure. Its large iron bars were twisted into fine, ornate shapes. There was a panel of strange buttons mounted on the wall next to the structure. Reaver pressed one, and it glowed blue.

"Aether." I hadn't meant to say it out loud. The last thing I wanted was to strike up a conversation with the asshole Demon, but I was unfamiliar with this magic and the machinery it powered.

"Yes."

A large wooden box A large wooden box descended into the cage, and its door opened with a loud clang.

"What is this contraption?" I asked.

"It's called a hoist."

The cage door opened and Reaver stepped inside, his piercing gaze fixated on me. "Are you coming?"

I hesitated, heart racing at the thought of getting into that monstrosity. "There's no way I'm risking my life by hopping in there."

"It's perfectly safe," he reassured me.

"Aether is failing this realm, just like the sun is failing mine. How do you know we won't get stuck in that thing?"

"Aether is much more powerful than the sun, since it comes directly from the Crystal Forest. Besides, Murmur hoards it."

"So, he leaves the rest of Raetia struggling as the aether fails them, just so he can be comfortable?"

He remained silent.

"Wow, your uncle is a jewel of a male." My smile was sickly sweet.

He pursed his lips. "Come."

"Nope."

He stepped out of the hoist and into my space. Before I could resist, he bent down to pick me up.

I recoiled and said, "Ok, I'll go, if it means you will stop carrying me around."

I couldn't help but inwardly groan at the look of self-satisfaction on his face.

I trudged into the hoist, tempted to flee before the doors shut, but he put his hand on my shoulder. "Don't be afraid, my Little Creature."

My little creature. I always felt a strange pull toward him when he called me "little creature" but to be called his was another thing entirely. Part of me wanted to be claimed by him so badly, while another part knew it would be too dangerous. I was tempted and torn between my own desires and better judgement.

My body went rigid as he leaned forward and punched a button on the wall. With a low mechanical whir, the box shuddered and lurched into motion. I jumped back, gripping his lapels in terror, my entire body tensed in anticipation. He looked down at me with a dark expression that sent a thrill of excitement through me.

I glared daggers at him and released my grip, only to firmly grasp the metal hand bar beside me. A loud ping echoed through the space as the hoist came to an abrupt halt.

The doors opened to a grand foyer of vaulted ceilings adorned with intricate stonework. He grasped my elbow and guided me through the large hallway, my feet sinking into lush carpeting as we went. The walls were painted a solemn gray with deep black trim, giving the space an air of elegance.

We stopped at a door that I could have sworn had not been there before. But with a wave of his hand, it opened slowly for us. It was impressive. I'd met many people with magical powers but none with his level of power.

We stepped inside, and I was filled with awe and admiration at the sheer magnificence of the space. Candle-lit sconces lined the walls and crystalline chandeliers shimmered throughout; the furniture made of shiny dark wood.

"Where are we?"

"This is where I live."

No wonder the place felt so masculine. The atmosphere was just as alluring as he was.

The opposite wall was more like one giant continuous window. You could see the Raetian city in all its splendor. My mouth dropped open, and like a moth to a flame, I walked straight to the window. Beautiful stone buildings piled on top of each other. The incredible aether-powered trolleys chugging along the streets. A moon in the sky. Blue lights everywhere. It was incredible.

"What is the name of this city?"

"Milania, the capital of our realm."

I turned around, finding Reaver taking off his jacket and loosening the neck tie. He was so handsome, but I told myself not to stare. I told myself to keep my gaze elsewhere, but it was hard.

"Sit down."

"I think I'd rather stand."

"I don't care what you want. Sit."

Goddess, I wanted to punch him in his ridiculously plump mouth and knock out his beautiful white teeth. "You are such a dipshit!"

The one-sided smirk was so attractive it made me irate.

"There's something I have to do."

"Oh yeah? And what's that?"

Reaver made his way to the panoramic windows and stared out at the city. I turned to do the same, though I was staring at him from my peripheral view. "You will not like it."

"I haven't liked anything since the moment you took me, asshole."

"I'm not sure you fully understand what it is I do for the King."

I scoffed. "He's no king."

He ignored me. "Murmur has tasked me with training you and making sure you know how to please."

My entire body went rigid, and I turned to face him. "I thought you brought me up here to save me from his minions training me," I spat venomously.

He matched my position, facing me head-on. "If I'd told you I was the one tasked with training you, would you have come up here?"

No, I wouldn't have. I bit my tongue, refusing to relent to his logic. Training. Sexual servitude. Fear made my throat dry up instantly. "I will never be a slave."

"You're already a slave to your mortal princess."

"No, I'm there willingly. I get paid. I'm well taken care of and I get to live in a castle, for fuck's sake."

He inched closer, and my heart sped up. "You may be there willingly, but you didn't choose the life you have. You're there because serving the royal family has been your family's legacy for generations. You don't think I can tell how unfulfilled you are? How much your eyes twinkle with excitement every time I'm around you? Or the way your face just beamed looking at my city through the window?"

Well, he had me there, but there was no way I'd confirm his suspicions. "I won't have sex with you."

He got closer, crowding me against the window. "You will."

"You're delusional."

"You will because of how fast your heart beats when I walk into the room."

"That's because you scare me!"

He smirked, tracing the line of my jaw with his fingertips. The gentleness of his touch sent shivers down my spine. His hand moved up to my cheek and he paused, brushing his thumb against my skin before twirling a single strand of hair around his finger and tucking it behind my ear. "Oh, but you will because I can smell your burning need for me whenever we're close." He buried his nose in my hair and took a deep breath. "You smell utterly delicious."

I took in a sharp breath and slammed my eyes shut, willing my arousal to go away, but it was futile. "I won't sleep with you." My voice came out much less convincing than I needed it to be.

"It's not that easy."

"What do you mean? No means no, asshole."

"We don't ascribe to those moral lines here. You're in a new world and it's imperative that you learn how to navigate it or you won't live much longer. This is not a life of gardens and healing elixirs. This is the lion's den and you are but a lamb."

"I. Will. Not. Have. Sex. With. You."

"If I don't fuck you, then someone else will. In fact several someones, and they won't do it here in a nice place. They'll take you to the dungeon where they'll gang-rape you and beat you to a pulp until you're completely broken. Body and spirit."

"You're lying."

"I have no reason to lie. I walked into the King's office and heard him instruct his guards to take you to the dungeon and do as they pleased. I'm saving you here."

"Then tell him we did it."

"He will check."

My throat went dry with shock and my stomach twisted revolted at the thought of this tyrannical king verifying that every heinous act had been carried out against me. Fury coursed through me like wildfire as I felt my hands ball into fists, every muscle of my body screaming out in defiance. "What the hell is wrong with you people?"

"I'm already breaking the rules as it is, bringing you to my chambers when every other prisoner is trained and tamed in the dungeon."

"Then why did you bring me up here?"

He hesitated for a moment. "Because I'm curious to know what you are."

"This again? I'm just a mortal."

"You don't smell like a mortal. You don't look like a mortal."

"Of course I look like a mortal."

"You have no idea, do you?"

"No idea of what?

But he didn't answer. He just looked away, undoing his cufflinks and rolling up his sleeves as he walked away to a bar where he poured amber liquid into two short glasses. My body stiffened as he came back, his hair shifting around his chiseled face and broad shoulders, his green eyes holding me hostage.

When he was but a few inches away, he stopped. I looked up into his face, keeping my spine erect and my chin held high because I refused to let him in on just how nervous he made me. He passed me a glass and without hesitation, I consumed its contents in one gulp, the warmth providing no solace to my anxiousness.

Reaver's voice was laced with a wicked fervor as his menacing figure loomed ever closer. His breath, hot and sticky on my neck, sent shivers of pleasure running down my spine as he whispered darkly in my ear, "Don't worry, Little Creature. I won't hurt you...in a bad way."

His fingers traced seductive trails up and down my body, igniting an inferno that threatened to consume me whole. I wanted him like nothing else before, hungering for the pain and pleasure that he promised.

"Hurt can never be good," I protested breathlessly.

"But when it brings pleasure so intense it makes everything else disappear, it becomes something entirely different," he murmured huskily into my skin.

Bloody hell. I could feel my erratic breath lifting my chest with noticeable force. It didn't escape his notice because he took a sip of his drink, his gaze never leaving mine, the promises in his eyes too much for me to bear. "It's okay to give yourself permission to enjoy everything I plan on doing to you, my Little Creature."

It was in that moment I understood I was defeated. He had me cornered and the world of pleasure he offered seemed irresistible. We were engrossed by a powerful, inexplicable connection. No matter how hard I tried to resist him, I knew deep down that I wouldn't be able to say no.

Besides, the alternative was being exploited by a band of wicked individuals.

Still, I was too stubborn to give in to this quickly. Teeth grinding, I glared. "Do. Not. Call. Me. That."

He smirked, devious and brilliant. "Would you prefer I call you a whore, a weak mortal with no chance of escaping her fate?"

My arm whipped out like a coiled spring, and my palm exploded against his cheek with the impact of a bomb going off. The world slowed down as I watched his face contort in agony before snapping to the side with a deranged force, followed by his body, as he flew halfway across the room, crashing against the wet bar. Decanters and bottles fell off, shattering into a thousand glass shards. An avalanche of amber liquid splattered all over the floor, spreading like blood over a battlefield.

I don't understand.

I stared at my hand, wide-eyed and wondrous, shocked by its steadiness, as if I hadn't displayed the strength of a powerful Mystic. Flickers of white, like tiny lightning bolts, covered my palm, traveling up my wrist and forearm.

My heart pounded and my mouth went dry as a million tiny sparks cascaded from my outstretched arm. They crept up my body, climbing my neck and shoulders like spiders, until my entire being was engulfed in this electric force. An excruciating pain overwhelmed me, and I crumpled to the ground, unable to control the violent spasms that wracked my body. My throat felt tight and no sound escaped as a powerful surge of energy lifted me off the floor and shot through me, coursing through my veins, invading my bones, and searing into my spirit.

Back arched and chest heaving, I floated, desperate to rub the pain off my skin, but the power had taken over, forcing my arms wide and my head to tip toward the ceiling.

"Reetah, what the fuck?"

His voice was distant and muffled, even though he was in the same room. "Reetah!"

"Ahhhh." My scream was dislodged, ripping through my vocal cords with the force of my terror.

My senses were on high alert, and I snapped my head down as I felt his approach. He lunged forward, arm outstretched, aiming for my ankle.

But before he could make contact with me, I unleashed a powerful wave of energy. He flew backward with a thud, crashing against the wall, held in place by an invisible force. With every thrust of energy from me, small fractures formed along the wall behind him.

A dark cloud spread from his body as he strained, eyes bulging and mouth twisting in pain. Tendrils of inky darkness began to pour out of him. The shadows seemed to pulse and writhe, attempting to overpower me. I could feel static electricity coursing through me, growing in strength with each passing moment. The intensity of our clash seemed to render him immobile as he stared at me with wide eyes, mouth agape in shock.

"Reetah! Stop this at once!"

"I'm not the one doing it!"

"Yes, you are. Control your power!"

I wanted to argue, tell him he was wrong, that I was a mortal, but the source of this power was undeniable. It came from deep inside me, an ancient place which had been sealed up my whole life and had suddenly opened, unleashing the secrets within.

Humbling. Awe-inspiring. Epic.

Darkness slammed into me, making me jolt. My eyes snapped to Reaver, his shadow magic pouring out of his chest, his fingers, his eyes. It made him look majestic and terrifying.

Despite his extraordinary power, my lightning, or whatever it was, continued to keep him pinned against the wall.

"Reetah! Focus."

Right. Focus. I needed to focus.

I closed my eyes and breathed, reining in the power. It resisted, but I kept at it, coaxing it like it was a child in need of assuaging.

The vibrations inside me mellowed, and I opened my eyes, watching as the bolt of white electricity retracted from Reaver, shortening until it reached me, where it plunged into the depths of my belly.

My feet hit the ground with a loud thud, knees buckling, a wave of exhaustion following close behind, forcing me to shut my eyes and curl up into the fetal position. Thankfully, Reaver's rug was more comfortable than most beds.

"Reetah." His voice came in a whisper, his fingers brushing the hair off my clammy forehead.

Too tired to speak, I cracked an eye open to look at him. He was crouched next to me, a strange look on his face as he stared at my arms, which I'd tucked under my cheek.

Reaver clasped my arm, and I didn't resist. He tugged my hand out from beneath me and raised it in front of my eyes.

A gasp escaped from my lips, filling my lungs with too much oxygen and making me lightheaded. I gazed at my once unblemished arm, which now bore dozens of small brands that spanned from my shoulder to wrist, like black ink etchings on paper. It didn't seem real.

I sat up in a flash, flexing both arms in front of me, a second gasp escaping when I spotted another set of the same sigils gracing my other arm. Tears welled in my eyes as a sob tore from my soul, recognition engulfing me with so much emotion, I wasn't sure I could withstand it.

"Do you know what they are?" Reaver asked, the deep bass in his voice somehow calming my frazzled nerves and bringing me back to the present.

I lifted my head to look at him, but tears were pooling in my eyes, making it difficult to see. I blinked them away, shaking my head slightly. My emotions were running rampant through me, pulsating with shock and wonder, and I couldn't control it any more than I could control my newfound power.

"Tell me what this is?" he pressed on, worry and impatience in his eyes.

I vaguely wondered why he would be worried, when it was clear he didn't give a shit about me, but I was too busy freaking out about everything that had happened in the last five minutes.

"Answer me, Reetah. Where do these brands come from?"

"Witch magic."

14

ITCH MAGIC.

I narrowed my eyes, staring at her awe-struck face, my mind racing as I made sense of what had happened.

One moment she'd slapped me, and the next I was crashing into the wall across the room, her hit carrying the strength of a Mystic.

I knew she wasn't mortal, but I hadn't expected her to be this powerful. Amazement filled me as I scanned her face, the effects of Murmur's violence gone from her beautiful face. She could now heal herself.

I couldn't resist and lifted her into my arms, placing her on my lap on the couch. When I rubbed small circles on her back, she stared at me with those big blue eyes, her back stiffening as she pulled away slightly.

"What are you doing?"

"What does it look like I'm doing?"

"Why are you being kind to me?"

"Would you prefer I go back to being a dick?"

Shaking her head, she gave me a small grin.

"Good. Now, relax."

Her hesitation was short-lived, and she snuggled up to me, her temple resting on my shoulder.

"I need you to talk and tell me everything you know."

"I already told you it's my family's magic."

"I've met several witches in my many years of life, and I know that wasn't the only thing happening to you."

Lifting her head, she looked at me, an edge of anxiety in her gaze. "I swear to you, Reaver, I'm not hiding anything. My mom comes from a long line of powerful witches, but she's only an earth witch. As the Stygian grows and infects the Crystal Forest, more and more of the witches in my family haven't been able to go through the empowerment, which is why we're now considered earth witches, which is basically a fancy term for healer."

"It seems you just went through yours."

"Yeah…" I said, still in disbelief.

"What about your father?"

She shifted in my lap, and I tensed as the friction made me harden. I ignored it, unwilling to sidetrack her from spilling all her family secrets.

"My father has no family."

"Everyone came from someone else."

"All I know is that he's not from my realm but from Volsci."

Volsci, the realm of thunder. Something in the back of my mind niggled at me, but I couldn't pinpoint it.

"Is he a Mystic?"

She shook her head. "For millennia, the rulers of Volsci forced his ancestors to become warriors. His kind had no choice but to serve Volsci's army, often chosen to do the most arduous battles or forced into becoming mercenaries. So they escaped, making the trek through the Crystal caves and begging the late King Urien to give them passage so they could seek asylum in the other realms. He granted their request, dividing their convoy into three equal units, one settling in Frentani, another in Lucania, and another here in Raetia. Over the years, just as the witches, more and more of them never came into their power, and as far as I know, my father is one of those who remained mortal."

Forced into becoming mercenaries.

Every muscle in me froze, and it became hard to swallow. This couldn't be.

"Reaver, what's wrong?"

It all made sense. My uncle's insistence I take not just the Frentanian Princess but her mortal lady's maid as well. The way she had drawn me to her from the beginning. An invisible pull I couldn't discern but was impossible to ignore. The way she came into her powers, provoked by rage. The bolts crackling all around her and maneuvering me as if I were but a puppet.

"Berserker."

"What?"

"You father comes from a long line of berserkers, as did my mother."

"What? But you're a Demon."

"Half a Demon. My father bedded one of his slaves and impregnated her. I'm the result of their tryst. After I was born, he refused to let her see me. Her rage and anguish were so profound it triggered her empowerment and she attacked him, revealing her abilities. My father and uncle restrained her. They caged her, controlling her mind in order to get her to do their dirty work, turning her into the most efficient and prolific killer this realm has ever seen."

"Controlling her mind? How?"

"The female that groomed you today."

"I don't follow."

"She's a mind bender, able to subdue people into doing her will. She's the one who does the taming."

I couldn't believe my ears. Such an unassuming older lady able to wield enough power to get anyone to do her bidding. "Is this why there are no guards in the dungeon?"

He nodded. "No need for guards when everyone remains submissive."

"Where is your mother now?"

I swallowed hard, my heart clutched in a vise of grief as memories of my mother filled me. I'd never met her but felt the bond we shared—the loss that forever connected us in life and death.

Reetah's ocean gaze was a beacon of truth. Like a floodgate of emotion, sorrow and pain rushed me. Her sheer beauty made me feel fragile, as if I wasn't a Demon who had cultivated the power to kill hundreds, but rather an innocent child who needed her protection. Tears brimmed in my eyes. "She gave up her life to end the cycle of suffering, and also to protect me from herself."

"Why from herself?"

"Because berserkers are notorious for losing their temper and destroying everything around them, friend or foe."

"Who told you she killed herself?"

"My father."

"And you believe him?"

I shrugged. "It's never been something I've dwelt on, but that was the day I promised myself I'd never experience emotion again."

Her gaze softened, but it wasn't with pity, which I despised, but with understanding. She cupped my face, and I let her, enjoying her warmth and the softness of her skin.

"No child deserves what happened to you, just like she didn't deserve to be used and kept away from her baby."

The blackness in my chest tore wide open, a gaping hole revealing my innermost feelings to this magnificent creature. She saw it all, and I let her, drowning in her beauty and the depth of her soul, which I could see clear as day, luminous and magnetic and loveable.

Grabbing her wrists, I pulled her hands from my face, bringing mine up to cup her soft pink cheeks. The little gasp that escaped her pouty mouth made me harden under her ass. Our eyes locked, and I felt a strange mixture of emotions. A part of me wanted to look away, but another part was drawn in by the intensity of our connection. The silence was heavy with unspoken words, yet somehow, we were communicating more than we ever had before.

With one look, I told her who I was under my cold and deviant exterior.

With one look, I told her I saw all of her, and that she'd never be able to hide herself from me.

With one look, I told her how much I wanted her.

And when her gaze darkened with understanding, I lunged.

REETAH

REAVER CRASHED HIS MOUTH ON MINE, and I welcomed his kiss with undiluted enthusiasm.

Yes, it was true he'd kidnapped me and even hurt me, but I saw right through it all, down to the sweet boy he once was, before his evil father robbed him of his mother and his innocence.

I surrendered to his dominance as he trailed his tongue over my lips and I opened to let him in. Fire burned in my belly and wetness pooled in my panties as my tongue came out to greet him and my hands fisted his silky raven hair.

He growled, and I felt it all the way down to my toes. I moaned in response before maneuvering over his lap until I straddled him, the hardness in his pants spurring me on.

Grinding against him, I murmured against his lips, "I'll do it."

He pulled away from me to look into my eyes. "Do what?"

I leaned in and whispered into his ear, "Have sex with you."

His brow furrowed as he studied me for a while before responding. "Why?

"Because I want to." Because I was done fighting this connection between us.

"I'm not a good man."

"It doesn't matter."

"Two hours ago it did, what changed?"

"Besides the fact that you were right about me not being mortal?"

He continued to stare at me without blinking, but said nothing.

"I'm done fighting with you. I'm tired of fighting...this," I said waving a hand between us.

I refrained from telling him I'd found comfort in him amidst this wretched world. That his voice had been my solace as I floated, consumed by white sparks and the pain of the marks branding into my skin. I didn't want to tell him my heart ached for him as he told me the terrible story of what happened to him and his mother, or the fact he was half berserker. And apparently, so was I.

My father had some explaining to do. Family secrets never led to anything good, and he'd deliberately left out our berserker history.

A swirl of absolute lust flashed in his eyes before he swept a hand into my hair and gripped, fisting it as he pushed my face closer to his. I gasped, surprised and turned on by his dominance.

As he kissed me, the raw heat that filled my body grew until I could feel nothing else. His tongue darted in and out of my mouth with unbridled fervor as mine met his eagerly. A groan slipped past both of us at the same time as I tangled my fingers in his hair, smiling as I traced a finger along the pointy angle of his ears. His rough stubble scraping against my smooth skin made me weak with desire.

Oh Goddess.

His big hands caressed the skin of my upper thighs, at the lacy bands attached to the garter, and he moaned his approval. "It seems I'll also get to undress you."

I couldn't stop gyrating atop him as his hand landed on my ass, squeezing hard, and making me whimper. He stood, and I held on, my arms wrapped around his neck and my tongue drawing circles over the delicious skin of his neck. I didn't know where he was taking me, but I didn't care. All I focused on was him. His large and muscular body making me feel protected, his big hands making me feel safe, and his tongue worshiping me.

He dropped me on a soft mattress, and I giggled as I bounced on it, a sound I was unused to producing.

"Get your giggles out now, because you won't be giggling in a minute when I devour you."

He was so damn sexy. "Get on with it, Demon."

His smile was wicked as he wasted no time undressing me. Boots first, then skirt as he straddled my hips. My eyes widened when he pulled out his dagger.

"Don't worry, baby, I won't hurt you. Unless you want me to."

By the Goddess, I wanted him to hurt me in the most uncouth and passionate ways.

With a swift glide of the blade, the bustier and breast wrap fell to my sides, my impossibly hard nipples staring right at him, and judging by the hunger in his eyes, he liked what he saw.

"Getting you dressed earlier today was torture."

"That bad, huh?" A small smile curved my lips as I relished the fact that I could have control over such a powerful man.

He let out a growl. "Dressing you without being able to taste you was excruciatingly torturous." He dove, clamping his mouth over one nipple, a hand squeezing the other. I gasped, arching my back in pleasure. A low moan, guttural and desperate, escaped his lips, as if he were a starving man getting the sustenance his life depended on. "Magnificent."

He was too much, and I loved it.

I pulled on the tie around his neck, letting out a small growl of frustration as my fingers struggled to undo it, lust and anticipation making them tremble. He chuckled darkly, swatting my hand away and undoing the tie while I unbuttoned his shirt as fast as I could. He straightened, ripping the shirt off his incredible torso, and throwing it on the floor to join our growing pile of clothing.

I glided both palms over his pecs, hard, with a smattering of dark hair. He watched me intently while I explored his impressive abs and that damn trail of hair leading right to the hardness I yearned for.

"Fuck," he hissed, moving my hands out of the way as he undid his belt buckle and slid it out of his pant loops with a loud snap that had me melting and wanting to submit to his every whim. "I should take my time with you, but I need to have you right now."

My head bobbed frantically in approval. "You can take your time with me later, Demon. Now, fuck me."

The grin on his face was deviant, though it disappeared the moment he ripped the lacy panties off my body with one hand.

He spread my legs wide, and I allowed it, captivated by the raw desire that flashed across his features. The sight of him was enough to make me even wetter.

Then he pulled out his impressive erection, and I moaned shamelessly loud. His erection was long, thick, and hard, and I wanted it inside me.

I wrapped my legs around his waist and pulled him to me, kissing him like his mouth was the fountain of life.

He grunted, and in one swift movement, thrusted inside.

"Oh Goddess!" I screamed, my toes curling with the onslaught of sensation his magnificent dick brought me. He stretched me and filled my emptiness completely. The orgasm hit me within seconds, surprising me because not even when I pleasured myself had I managed to orgasm so quickly. But all of our sexual tension had finally found an outlet.

His movements became uneven before he stopped altogether, pulling out of me. He jerked himself above my stomach, ropes of his cum landing on my trembling skin.

I stared at the droplet of his seed on the crown of his cock and wiped it off before bringing my finger to my lips and sucking. I closed my eyes, reveling in his taste, tangy and salty, and unlike anything else. I wasn't a virgin, but I'd never felt so at ease with my past lovers as I did with Reaver.

I ran my finger through the pool of cum on my belly, swirling it as I stared up at him, his dark gaze taking me in with a strange gleam in his eye, akin to awe.

I smiled sweetly at him, before bringing my finger back to my mouth and sucking on it as I moaned, making a show of how much I enjoyed it. How much I enjoyed him.

Leaning down with a ferocious look on his face, he wrapped a hand around the back of my head, bringing my face inches from his. "You like to tease, don't you, baby?"

I smiled coyly. "I don't know what you're talking about."

His wolfish grin sent shivers down my spine. "Don't worry, I will relish punishing you for your teasing ways."

And punish, he did.

REAVER

SHE WAS UNREAL.

So beautiful and genuine, with an unrestrained passion which rivaled mine.

She was in captivity, but she was no captive. She never let herself break, and beyond her strength, I could also see a desire to be wild. I saw a female who didn't fit the persistently positive world she lived in. A girl who craved dark waters. A girl who didn't shy away from the world I'd thrust her into.

Reetah was a survivor, and beyond that she was a berserker, and this spoke to the part of me I could no longer deny. I was a berserker, and though I didn't have the powers of one, my mother did, and she deserved for me to embrace myself wholly and without fear and judgment.

Heat blazed in my body as I watched her lick my cum off her fingers, the glint in her eye telling me she loved teasing me.

Which meant I had no choice but to punish her with pleasure.

I pushed myself up to standing, making quick work of ridding myself of my pants, socks, and shoes. I didn't miss the way her eyes grew and her cheeks flushed as she took in my naked form, my dick once again hard and ready for her. This time, though, I'd take my time and get creative with her punishment.

Lying on the bed, I weaved my fingers behind my head. "Get on top of me."

She smiled with glee and did as I instructed, a fresh wave of her arousal hitting my nose and making my cock even harder. Straddling me, she simply moved back and forth over the smooth skin of my erection, her wetness causing the most delicious friction. I held my breath through it all, working hard on resisting the urge to slam inside her. Instead, I focused on each mesmerizing detail of her face as she pleasured herself.

When she ground on me faster and faster, I put a hand under each of her ass cheeks, and flipped her over before sliding atop her gorgeous body, still clad in the garter belt, though the panties were long gone.

She blew a strand of hair off her face, frowning as if displeased with me for interrupting her pleasure-seeking efforts.

Good.

"Open your legs."

She crossed her arms across her breasts, pouting. "Why didn't you let me finish?"

Her pout was adorable. "Because you come when I tell you to come. Now put your arms above your head and keep them there."

She pursed her lips in displeasure, though her eyes lit up with undeniable excitement.

I made my way down her body, my tongue leaving trails of wetness on her skin, until my face was level with her pussy. It was beautiful and delicate, the short hairs atop her pelvic bone golden like her head. Parting her with my thumbs, I inhaled, her scent so sweet I never wanted to pull away. Closing my eyes, I relished in all that was Reetah, my tongue darting out to lick at her clit. She cried out, her hips lifting off the mattress and her thighs clamping around my head. I pinned them under my forearms and continued my task, sucking on her most sensitive spot.

"It's too much!" She pulled on my long hair like they were reins she needed to hold on to, lest she fell into the void where her climax awaited.

Which only meant I had to push her to the brink.

I smiled, taking her wrists with one hand. "I won't tolerate disobedience." I placed her hands against the headboard. "You leave me no choice but to make sure you can't escape your punishment."

Letting out a tendril of shadow, I bound her wrists to it. She squirmed, but didn't refute, instead opening her legs wide as if beckoning me to resume my tongue's ministrations on her pussy.

My little creature liked to play the game and who was I to deny her the best match of her life? One where I wrung out all of her desire.

I repositioned myself and focused on licking up her slit and circling her clit with my hot tongue. She screamed and cried with pleasure, her entire body covered in sweat, making her skin glisten.

And right as she was about to explode, I pulled away.

"What the fuck, Demon?" She seethed, and I chuckled.

"I told you I decide when you get to come."

Rage whirled in her eyes as she tried to bring her hands down, which only made me tighten the shadow encircling her wrists. She huffed in exasperation. "You're mean."

I smiled. "And you love it." I kissed her deeply, and she let out a whimper so sexy it was an aphrodisiac.

"Can you please let me come soon?"

I threw my head back and laughed because her pleas were as adorable as they were fierce. "The more you want it, the less I'll give it to you," I whispered huskily, rubbing my nose on hers with surprising intimacy.

A moment later, I released her arms, calling the shadows back into my body. With her hands now on my chest, she pushed me away, her gaze searing into me. "Why? Why would you do that?"

"Because I want to drive you so wild you lose your mind." I expected her to call me cruel, but she had no answer. Or rather, her answer was to wrap her legs around me and pull me in with a scorching kiss and a demand to drive her crazy.

I churned my tongue inside, loving her moan as she tasted herself on my lips and tongue.

I positioned myself at her entrance, loving the way her breath hitched when she felt the crown of my cock.

The realization that I wanted this more than anything shocked me but I was in too deep to fear what this meant, not only for my heart but my job, and my relationship with my uncle, as it was becoming impossible for me to imagine being able to live with myself if she became a sex slave, doomed to pleasure bad and filthy men for the rest of her life. The thought alone threatened to ruin the moment, so I let it go, refocusing on the beautiful female staring up at me with expectant eyes. I inched in little by little, thrusting in and pulling out, before rocking in deeper until she welcomed it all, down to the base.

Her impossible tightness brought with it an ache I relished. "Baby, you're so tight."

Baby. A term of endearment I'd never used on anyone before. Come to think of it, I'd never used terms of endearments on a single soul; the hardening of my heart starting when I was a mere child, without a mother to teach me the art of tenderness.

But Reetah unearthed things in me I didn't know existed. She brought out a caring side that, for the first time in my life, made me consider someone else's needs besides my own.

The need to protect her, care for her, keep her safe. It was overwhelming, but I welcomed it, letting it make my chest puff out with the fullness of it all.

"Look at me," I demanded, my heart seizing when her big eyes, blue as a summer sky, stared up at me with so much affection. Affection I didn't deserve, but wouldn't dare turn down.

My lips found hers and I kissed her with a tenderness unfitting the monster I was. Her pillowy lips welcomed me, her wee tongue tangling with mine, spurring me to thrust deeper, though I kept my pace languid. With the overbearing sexual tension between us burned out by that first fuck, which was short but intense, we now had all the time in the world to explore one another. Which was what I planned on doing.

"You feel so good." Her pants were sexy as hell, along with that gorgeous hair sprawled all over my pillows. My bed had never looked so good.

As the pooling of pressure at the base of my spine increased, I couldn't help but close my eyes, the onslaught of pleasure taking over.

My eyes reopened when I felt the warmth of her hand on my cheek. "Look at me," she beckoned, and I heeded her call, gazing deeply into her depths as I rocked into her with more purpose.

She smiled sweetly, though the rest of her face showed how turned on she was. I kissed her smiling lips, moaning into her mouth as I succumbed to the powerful force threading us together. A wealth of emotion and connection so mighty, it caused my entire body to vibrate.

"Are you okay, my gorgeous Demon?" she asked, her brows furrowing as she took in the incessant quaking of my body.

Searing heat exploded inside me, my breath ceasing from the shock of the burn. "Fuck," I bellowed, going down to my forearms because my hands shook too much to hold me up. Reetah's eyes grew big, and in them, I saw the same sparks from earlier. Her arms hooked around my neck, her legs squeezing my hips and refusing to let go. I fucked her hard but tender, angry and sweet, slow and fast.

Her hair floated above the pillow, and I felt my eyes widen in awe and surprise.

"What's happening?" she panted, still holding on to me and matching the bucking of her hips with the beat of my thrusts.

I sat back on my haunches, bringing her with me. Her body fit against mine perfectly, and I reveled in the sensation of her bouncing on my shaft.

I embraced her body tightly as I tugged her hair with my other hand, bringing her face closer to mine. Our mouths connected in a passionate exchange of lips, teeth, tongues, and wetness that felt like magic.

This went beyond your everyday sex. This was intense, it was sultry, it was something special, and it was simply breathtaking.

A profound sense of weightlessness hit me, making my stomach dip as a heavy electrical charge swirled in and around me. Reetah yelped, and I opened my eyes, the sight of her floating hair and berry-kissed Reetah yelped, and I opened my eyes, the sight of her floating hair and berry-kissed lips filling me with an overwhelming sense of longing. Of belonging.

The fear in her eyes snapped me out of my Reetah-induced haze, my senses grasping that her hair wasn't the only thing floating.

We were floating, wrapped in a cloud of sparks. They crackled and danced across her eyes, hair, and skin, seeping into every part of me which was connected to her. The heat in my body grew painful, an unfathomable pressure making me feel like I was about to blow up from the inside out, as our tangled bodies soared above the bed.

Our eyes remained locked through it all, entranced.

"Reaver! Your eyes."

I frowned. "What is it?"

"They're sparking red!" Her face beamed, her smile so bright it made my heart sing. She broke eye contact, but only for a second as she stared at my chest. I looked down, shocked to see my entire body alive with red lightning.

The sensation could only be described as transcendental. I let go of her back and hair to cup her face, and as expected, we remained connected, wrapped in an electrical cocoon. One more look into her eyes told me I wasn't the only one who understood what was happening, as the pieces of the puzzle fell, fitting with an effortlessness which had been foreign to my life up to this point.

We kissed and fucked. We mated, and I became utterly and irrevocably besotted with my little creature.

And through the forging of our bond, the berserker in me awoke.

REETAH

E WAS MY MATE.

The one who would have my soul for the rest of my life.

And he was filled with lightning like me. Like his mother. Only his were red.

My heart swelled with joy and ecstasy, and I could no longer contain the tears streaming down my face as he pounded into me with ferocity, faster than ever before. His grunts and growls felt like thunder in my veins, driving me to an uncontrollable crescendo of pleasure that threatened to overwhelm me.

"Reetah," he bellowed, voice raspy and laden with pent-up, well, everything.

In minutes, he had found his mate, had undergone his empowerment into becoming a berserker, and judging by the way he fucked me, and the lust shooting from his every pore, this was the best sex of his life.

I knew it was mine.

"Sun melt me!" I screamed as the most earth-shattering orgasm slammed into me, every nerve in my body exploding with the hit.

"Yes, fuck, yes!" he said, before stiffening, his pumps losing their rhythm as he joined me in bliss, spurting his hot seed inside me.

Thoughts about safety and pregnancy crossed my mind, but they were fleeting. He was my mate. Life as we knew it before this moment no longer mattered.

I would die for him, and he would die for me. This, I didn't doubt because I felt it in my soul.

Holding each other, we panted as our powers ebbed and our bodies lowered back to the bed.

We lay front to front, his erection still inside me, and by the Goddess, I didn't want him to pull out. Not ever.

His thumb swept the tears drying on my cheeks. "You are everything I'd ever wanted but never imagined being worthy enough to receive. I still don't think I'm worthy, but here we are."

I smiled, playing with the scruff on his cheek. "You deserve all of this and more, mate."

His inhale was deep as he shook his head in disbelief. "Bloody hell, this is all so—"

"Crazy?"

He chuckled. "To say the least."

It made so much sense now. The way he drew me in, even when all I saw was a shadow in the light. The way he scared me and yet, didn't, as if I could sense the bond even though he'd taken me and held me captive. My stomach soured when my reality crashed back into my mind. I was his captive, and he was supposed to train me as a sex slave. This was why he'd offered me sex, to prevent Murmur's minions from violating me.

"Hey, look at me." He gently grabbed my chin, forcing me to face him. He stared into my eyes, and I could see the conflict within his. "You're mine now."

His words made my heart soar, though the heaviness remained. My head bobbed in reluctant agreement. "We can just tell him I'm your mate."

He shook his head. "You can't."

"Why not?"

"Because he'll use you as leverage to get me to do his bidding."

"What exactly does this mean?"

"It means that everything has changed. My priority is no longer with him, but with you, and when he realizes this, he won't be pleased."

"I get it, but we have kickass superpowers now."

He chuckled. "Kickass?"

I smiled and nodded. "Yup. Do you think I'll get a Watcher?"

He threw his head back with laughter. "If you do I should too, after all, I'm only half Demon." His smile diminished as he played with a lock of my hair. "No one can know what you are."

I propped myself on an elbow. "Are you saying I can't use my abilities?"

"That is precisely what I'm saying."

I glowered at him. "How is that fair? I spend my whole life powerless, and now that I have the power of two practically dead magical lines, I can't explore it?"

"Not until we figure out how to get away from my family. I will not let you end up like my mother, which is exactly what they'll do to you if they find out what you can do. You'll become a weapon of mass destruction, and they'll rip you away from me."

The pained look on his face made me gulp. "What are we going to do, then? Your uncle is an ancient king of hell. He's mighty and will never allow us to just walk away. We'll never be free of him."

"Then I will do what I must."

"Which is?"

"I must kill the king of hell."

Thank you for reading!
This story will continue as part of the Realms of Anathema series, filled with dark gothic romance and epic fantasy.
Sign up for my newsletter to get all the updates:
https://bit.ly/3JA

ACKNOWLEDGMENTS

Writing this book was as scary as it was exhilarating and I wouldn't have been able to do it without the help of many.

To my family, thank you for your undying support and suggestions on plot and character names. I love you.

To my PA Kelly for all the help when all I could handle was the writing. I also want to thank you for your honesty when giving me critiques. They only made the book stronger.

To my friends Katie, Julia, Christie, and Olivia for always having my back and watching my kid so I could write!

To Christine Hutton for the countless hours of brainstorming with me as I figured out this new gothic fantasy world.

To my beta readers Marina, Crystal, Christine, Alexandra, Haley, and Chanel. Couldn't have done it without you!

To my website guy, Manuel, you are the best!

Zainab, I love you, my dear!

And to Nisha, my go to girl for promoting my book babies. Thank you!

And more than anything, thank you to the readers for trusting and believing in me!

ABOUT THE AUTHOR

Vale grew up with the elves and the faeries and still looks for dragons in every land she visits.
She went to college twice, getting degrees in theater and psychology because she's crazy like that.
Now, she sips tea in the mountains, writing love books full of passion, pain and magic. Her books will take you places where your heart will be ripped out, before being put back together better than before.
She writes contemporary romance, dark romance, and epic fantasy.

She loves to connect with her readers.

Let's be friends!
Visit my website:
https://valeravenna.com/